DEADLY LIES

A GIA SANTELLA CRIME THRILLER
BOOK 15

KRISTI BELCAMINO

LIQUID MIND PUBLISHING

Copyright © 2022 by Kristi Belcamino. All rights reserved. No part of this publication may be copied, reproduced in any format, by any means, electronic or otherwise, without prior consent from the copyright owner and publisher of this book.

Liquid Mind Publishing
This is a work of fiction. All characters, names, places and events are the product of the author's imagination or used fictitiously.

GIA SANTELLA CRIME THRILLER SERIES

Enjoying the Gia Santella series? Scan below to order more books today!

Vendetta

Vigilante

Vengeance

Black Widow

Day of the Dead

Border Line

Night Fall

Stone Cold

Cold as Death

Cold Blooded

Dark Shadows

Dark Vengeance

Dark Justice

Deadly Justice

Deadly Lies

PROLOGUE

We were more than 400 feet up in the air, balanced on a rickety metal platform on top of the highest roller coaster I'd ever seen.

His dark form remained a silhouette as he grew closer, the hem of his trench coat flapping in the wind behind him. We were so high up I could see the Golden Gate Bridge across the Bay glowing in the night sky behind him.

The wind whipped up a small maelstrom, sending long strands of my hair in front of my eyes, but I ignored it, keeping both arms straight in front of me, both hands wrapped around the Glock 26 that I had pointed at his chest.

It took everything I had not to squeeze the trigger.

I'm not supposed to kill him.

An image of god-fearing women in high-heeled pumps and gloves kneeling in church came back to me.

They were all praying for the soul of this piece of shit who was close enough now that I could kill him easily with one shot. But I held back.

I'd promised I'd try not to kill him.

I like to keep my promises.

But damn it. He was making that really hard.

I was shivering even though I had on my thick leather motorcycle jacket. He must be colder. I crept even closer. That's when he stepped out of the shadow into the light, and I nearly squeezed the trigger. He was holding a gun.

It was pointed at me.

"Put the gun down," I yelled.

He was a bit unsteady on his feet, and the barrel of the gun was wobbling around a bit. He probably couldn't hit me, but I didn't want to take any chances.

He took a step forward.

"Whoa!" I said and backed up. "Tell me right now why I shouldn't kill you. Put down the gun, or I'll be forced to. And believe me, I want to do it."

"I'm not going to prison," he said.

In the distance, I heard the first wail of sirens. Out of my peripheral vision far below me, I saw a line of squad cars with their lights on coming down the freeway toward the amusement park.

I exhaled loudly and tried to control the urge to take his head off right then and there.

"Listen you piece of shit," I said. "I want you dead. People like you, who prey on the weak and helpless, you don't deserve to live. You have destroyed entire families. As far as I can see—and I've looked—you don't have any redeeming qualities."

"Fuck you, you dyke bitch."

I actually laughed out loud.

"That the best you got?" I asked.

He was trembling with rage. Sweat poured down his brow. His black and gray hair was blowing to one side, revealing how thin it was. His ruddy skin was ashen in the carnival lights. He didn't look so fucking powerful now.

He was no longer the man who made people cower when he barked orders at restaurants and berated anyone and everyone. He was no longer the boss who slipped his hand up his secretary's skirts and threatened to fire them if they didn't put up with it. He was no longer the cheating husband who flaunted his mistresses and endless string of prostitutes in front of his long-suffering wife.

He was no longer the man who had coldly ordered four murders that had devastated four families.

Nope. He was no longer any of those things.

He looked like a desperate, scared, and pathetic little man.

Which is exactly what he was.

"Time's almost up for you," I said.

My finger was twitching—eager to squeeze the trigger and end the life of this waste of sperm.

But I'd made a promise.

"I'm not going to prison."

"You are," I said in a matter-of-fact voice. "It won't be so bad in prison."

"You are going to die," he said. The barrel of his gun wobbled around wildly. I stayed in my stance, trying to keep my weary arms steady.

The sirens were getting closer now. Out of the corner of my eye, I saw the line of cars pull into the amusement park's far entrance.

"You really think you are superior to everyone else, don't you?" I asked. I was genuinely curious. "And you really think you are invincible?"

"I am." His voice was smug. I could blow his fucking head off in two seconds, yet he was still cocky as fuck.

The squads had stopped below the base of the roller coaster.

I heard the hum of the elevator to our left being summoned.

"They'll be up here in less than five minutes."

"It will be too late," he said.

He gave a blood-curdling primal scream as he pulled the trigger.

1

I leaned my back against the wall and watched Rose through the crowded room.

She was perched on the edge of an emerald green velvet ottoman listening intently to another young woman speak.

Darling's massive and opulent living room was filled with people holding drinks and laughing and talking. The soft sounds of Marvin Gaye could barely be heard under the chatter. The low lights infused faces with a soft glow. A glittering chandelier in the center of the room was turned down low.

The party spilled out of the room and through the French doors onto the patio. Just beyond, the pool was lit up, turquoise blue and shimmering.

Everyone was dressed up except Rose.

Even me. Dante had ordered me to wear my knee-length leather dress with the cap sleeves. It hugged my curves without showing any flesh. I didn't argue. I loved butter soft leather. Unlike some of the dresses he made me wear, this one was comfortable and didn't feel all that different from wearing my beloved leather pants and a worn, soft T-shirt.

When I told Rose I'd be dressing up for the party, she looked at me without answering.

Later, she came out of her guest room at Darling's wearing a black tank top and charcoal gray cargo pants. Her long black hair fell down her back in a shiny sheet. Her huge black eyes and naturally red lips didn't need any makeup. Her dark skin was flawless.

"You look nice," she said about my dress.

I just walked up and hugged her. I was trying not to cry.

The party was her goodbye party.

I'd had her for a month. Four long, glorious weeks of catching up.

We'd spent some of it talking about her father.

We cried together remembering Nico and how we'd lost him to Alzheimer's long before we'd lost him to death.

More than a few nights were spent curled up on the couch in my hotel suite watching movies. Mostly, she sat in the living room and read all day. I asked her several times if she wanted to go out, but she would shake her head no.

Dante was with us the first two weeks. He and I had been busy with hotel business. We'd finally renovated the hotel the way we wanted to. Dante launched the re-opening of the restaurant and was planning to come back next month for a larger party.

Wayne, his husband, had flown up, and we'd spent a few nights at restaurants in North Beach, eating Italian food and drinking wine and talking late into the night until the managers kicked us out.

My heart was full. It had been a long time since I'd felt this much peace and love in my life.

But now Rose was leaving me again.

She missed her boyfriend. She missed her dog.

She missed her life without me.

I'd tried to argue, but she just looked at me and said, "There's someone out there killing young girls. What would you do?"

I gave her a slow nod.

I had been raised in a fairly normal house and had a fairly normal childhood. And yet, I still had blood on my hands.

Rose had been raised with murder and violence and death as a constant companion.

She'd only found peace once she'd accepted that she was born to be a killer.

I could never understand. I could only love her as she was and be there for her in every possible way.

She had not needed me for years.

But one night in the hotel room, she had wept about the lives she had taken and the role she felt she needed to play in life.

"You don't have to live this way," I told her. "You can have a normal life."

But even as I said it, we both knew it was a lie.

Now, watching her from across the room, I loved how she didn't feel the need to fit in. And the irony was, that even without makeup or fancy clothes, she was easily the most striking woman in the room. And Darling had some really beautiful friends with exquisite taste. Their makeup, hair, clothing and accessories were always perfect. I'd never seen one of Darling's tribe of friends dressed casually.

It was the way Rose held herself. So poised and confident for someone so young.

She was wise beyond her years.

I sat in the corner and must've given off a vibe because everyone let me be.

Or probably, more likely, Darling had told everyone to give me space.

She knew my heart was breaking.

At one point I walked over and joined Rose, scooting onto the edge of the ottoman.

Darling's two fancy-ass, expensive-as-fuck dogs were on the couch on either side of the woman Rose had been talking to.

She was stroking one's fur absentmindedly. The other had its head on her lap. So cute.

"I'm Gia," I said to her.

"Clara," the young woman said. Her infectious smile lit up her face, and she had striking green eyes against dark skin.

"You guys have been deep in conversation all night," I said. "Looked intense."

They both laughed.

"We were actually talking about rescue dogs," Clara said and reached over to scratch one of the dog's heads. "I'm studying law and working as a paralegal, so I'm not home enough to have one yet, but I'm counting the days until I can get my own dog."

Darling came over.

"I see you've met my grandniece, Clara," she said, pulling up a chair. "She's going to do big things. Change this country."

The young woman gave a nervous laugh and said, "If only all of us could live up to how Darling sees us; the world would be a better place."

"Honey, you are going to change the world. I have no doubt." Darling turned to me. "Valedictorian of her class."

I nodded, impressed.

Another woman nearby reached over and plucked a piece of cheese off a platter on the table by us.

"I love this cheese!" she said.

"Me too," Darling said.

"It is stinky though," the woman said.

People laughed.

"This is Kat," Darling said and introduced us.

"I have a funny story about stinky cheese," Kat said.

She told us that a divorcing couple was arguing over who should get the house. The husband had more money, and so he was able to force the woman out. Shortly after the wife moved out the man noticed an awful smell. He searched high and low for the source of the smell and couldn't find it. He brought in professionals and they were at a loss. Finally, he decided to sell the house because he just couldn't hack the smell anymore. All the people who came to look at it left, horrified because of the smell. Finally, his real estate agent told him he was just going to have to sell the house at a loss. He agreed.

As soon as the house was reduced in price, a real estate agent called up, and said she'd buy the house sight unseen.

"I have to disclose that there's a major odor issue," the husband's agent said.

"That's fine. Just draw up the paperwork. I don't want a long escrow."

A month later the wife moved into the house she'd just bought. The first thing she did was take down the circular curtain rods and throw them in the trash. She'd unscrewed the decorative ends and stuffed smelly cheese inside.

Everyone listening to the story burst into laughter, Clara especially. Her laughter was infectious.

Right after, her phone chirped. She looked down and frowned, then stood. "Excuse me for a second."

As she walked off toward the patio, I gave Darling a look.

She rolled her eyes. "She's the smartest person I know except when it comes to the men in her life."

I shot a look at Rose.

"What? Don't look at me. Damon and I are taking a break."

"You're leaving to go see him in the morning."

She scoffed. "Just to get my dog back."

But I was worried. I knew they truly loved each other, but I didn't think they were good for one another. I reminded myself that it was none of my business.

Darling was watching Clara as she paced out by the pool.

"Excuse me," she finally said and got up.

Rose yawned.

"You can go to bed," I said. "Darling will understand. You have an early start."

"You sure?"

I smiled. "Go on. I'll tell her you've gone to bed. Sneak out now."

She smiled and headed toward the back hall of the bedrooms.

My heart hurt as I watched her go.

By this time tomorrow, she'd be back in Florida.

I saw Darling out by the pool talking to Clara. Then a third woman joined them.

She was older, maybe in her early forties. She looked like an older version of Clara. I assumed it must be her mom. She didn't look happy.

Clara shrugged and gestured toward her phone.

Then the three came back in.

"Rose said to say goodbye. I sent her to bed. She has to be up at four to head back to the city for her flight."

Darling nodded. "Clara has to leave now anyway."

"Everything okay?" I asked.

"It's a long story," the woman said and smiled.

"A long story that has nothing to do with you," her mother quipped.

"I'm Gia," I said and stuck out my hand.

"Alisha Parks." Her grip was firm and her smile genuine. "I've heard so much about you."

I immediately recognized her name. She was a longtime friend and sorority sister of Darling's.

"Same," I said. "I can't believe we haven't met before now."

"I think we were both out of the country at different times," she said.

I remembered Darling had mentioned that Alisha Park's husband was a diplomat in Singapore.

"Are you living back in the States now or just on a visit?"

"Home for good," she said. "Thank god. I missed my tribe."

Darling nodded. "Mmmhmm. Wasn't the same without Alisha around."

It wasn't the first time I envied Darling's close knit group of friends.

I had my close friends: Dante, Darling, and Danny. (Obviously, you had to have a name that starts with a "D" to be my friend. Lol.)

But they were not just friends; they were family.

I'd never had a big group of close girlfriends.

I wasn't sure why. Maybe because I wasn't into shopping and gossip and soccer vans.

Yeah, that was probably it.

Darling was speaking quietly to people, and I noticed groups were leaving. She must have told them the party was over.

I went up to her. "I'm sneaking off now. Thank you."

"I'll see you in the morning."

"You don't have to get up to see us off."

She gave me a sideways irritated look.

"Fine," I said.

I learned a long time ago to never argue with that woman.

2

Not only was Darling up early, but she was dressed to the nines—as always—and had breakfast waiting for us.

Rose had dark circles under her eyes and was quiet, sipping her black coffee and nibbling on a cinnamon cardamom scone Darling had baked.

Then it was time to go.

Rose fell into Darling's large embrace and stayed there a long time. Darling was patting her back and making eyes at me over the top of her head. I wasn't sure what she was trying to convey, but she leaned down and said into Rose's ear, "Don't you ever forget Miss Rose that you have two mamas here in the Bay Area—me and Gia. We love you like you are our own flesh and blood, and don't you ever forget it!"

Darling's voice was soft but fierce.

Rose nodded her head and pulled back.

Without looking at me, she headed straight to the front door. I went over and kissed Darling's cheek. "Thanks, Darling."

Darling put her hands on her hips. "We're family."

"I know."

"Don't you spend a second worrying about that girl. I don't."

"You don't?"

"Nuh uh. She is stronger than the two of us put together—physically, emotionally, and mentally."

I sighed. "I hope you're right."

Darling lifted one eyebrow and I laughed.

Darling was always right.

I'd taken my newest car—a Maserati SUV—up to Darling's house in Mill Valley in the Marin headlands.

I didn't want my driver, Tony, to drive this far this early in the morning.

He was an ex-convict with a gold tooth and gold heart.

I'd bought the SUV a few weeks before when Rose came to town so I had something to drive to show her around and take her places. During her stay, we'd taken short weekend getaways. Even though my hotel room was a suite, it felt small for the two of us. We'd gone to Fort Bragg up the coast for a few days, to Calistoga to visit Dante while he was in town checking on his restaurants, and to Sacramento to tour the capitol.

I'd offered the car to Rose to use while she was there, but she had zero interest in leaving the room. It was only because of my insistence that we take the small trips that we left at all.

I was worried about her. I knew she was still grieving the loss of her father. Hell, I was still grieving his loss and always would be. But this was something else. She seemed distracted.

Now, in the car, I reached over and squeezed her hand.

"You okay?"

She smiled, and it lit up her face.

"Yeah. I'm excited to see Damon and Dylan."

I returned her smile.

"I'm so glad."

Then her smile disappeared.

"Gia, I don't want you to worry about me."

I took a deep breath and nodded. "I'm going to try my best. It would help if you could maybe keep in touch a bit more…"

She winced.

Fuck. I wasn't asking that much.

"I will when I can."

"Okay," I said.

But she wasn't done yet.

"Damon and I are going to be off the grid."

I waited.

"I bought a sailboat, and we're heading toward the Bermuda Triangle. That's where I think the person working with the Sultan is living," she said. "We're going to come in the back door."

I nodded.

The Sultan had been a cult leader who brainwashed young girls into being sex slaves. He sacrificed several of them. And endlessly taunted Rose.

It was only when she was forced with the decision of whether or not to kill him that he revealed he was her own brother.

And she killed him anyway.

I knew her new adventure was dangerous, but there was nothing I could say to stop her.

At the airport, I dropped her off at the curb. I got out and hugged her tightly.

"I love you, Gia," she said and gave me a smile that melted my heart.

"I love you, sweet girl."

It was what her father had always called her.

She smiled and walked away without answering.

BACK AT THE HOTEL, my suite felt empty without Rose and her things, but I dove into some hotel business I'd put off during her visit, and before I realized it, the sky out my window had turned a dark blue.

I ordered a salad and fish from room service. I had been focusing on eating healthy and exercising for the past month while Rose was there.

I hadn't really had alcohol since Anthony came to town and took us all out to dinner.

He was back in Washington, DC now in his new role as senator.

He promised to split his time between there and here, but for the first legislative session, he said he needed to be there to learn the ropes.

I hated to admit that I missed him. But he said he would be back in town this weekend.

I decided to forego the red wine and save it for dinner with him.

My dinner was amazing—Dante luring the city's top chef to our restaurant not only benefited the hotel; it benefited me personally. After I ate, I curled up on my couch and tried to watch a Spanish film that had been lauded at the Cannes film festival.

But I couldn't concentrate and turned it off.

Finally, the loneliness I'd been keeping at bay hit me hard.

My willpower was gone.

I ordered a pack of Dunhill blue cigarettes and two bourbons from room service—two items that I made sure the hotel stocked after Dante and I bought it.

I told room service to leave everything in my private hallway and to text me when they'd been delivered.

I was wearing only a tight tank top and my underwear and didn't feel like getting dressed just to answer the door.

A wave of overwhelming sadness overcame me.

I swallowed. It was a life I'd chosen.

I'd made a decision to live this life. It didn't mean that I'd always be alone. I had friends who were more precious than any blood relatives.

And I had two amazing men in my life who let me be me.

But still I found myself alone more often than not.

And so I was weak. I would tamp down the loneliness in ways I'd always done.

I wouldn't spend every last dime or sleep with every cute boy, but I would turn to vices that never did me any good—nicotine and alcohol.

Thinking this, I called room service back and told them to bring me an entire bottle of bourbon and a bucket of ice.

A few minutes later, I'd made myself a drink and was out on my deck wrapped in a blanket.

I stayed there a long time, drinking and smoking and watching the fog roll in under the Golden Gate Bridge.

3

I woke at noon with a hangover.

When would I learn?

Drowning my sorrows in booze and cigarettes had worked a lot better when I was younger.

Now, I felt good for about two hours and then paid for it for about ten.

I popped some ibuprofen and made some strong coffee.

Taking my coffee and grabbing my Dior sunglasses, I went back out on my deck. It was a beautiful day—blue skies and warm sun.

I sat in my deck chair and put up my feet. For some reason a memory of my mother came to me, and I thought of her and how excited she used to be when she'd take us to San Francisco and got her first glimpse of the Golden Gate bridge. No wonder seeing it still filled me with awe after all this time.

My phone rang.

Darling.

"Hey, doll," I answered.

"Gia, something bad has happened."

I stood up, alarmed.

Rose.

"It's Clara."

For a minute my mind was blank.

The young woman from the party.

Before I had a chance to ask what was wrong, Darling was explaining.

"Her mama just called. Clara and her friends went out to a club last night and never came home."

"*None* of them came home?"

"Not a one. There were four of them. They aren't answering their phones or texts either. No activity on social media since late last night at the club."

"Have you—" I began.

"We already talked to the police and the hospitals and even the damn morgue," Darling said.

The three places I was going to suggest.

"I don't suppose any of them have Find My Phone connected to their parent's cell phone accounts?"

"Nope," Darling said. "I asked."

As she spoke, I was in my bedroom pulling on cargo pants. "What can I do?"

"We're going to Clara's apartment in the Sunset district."

"I can head to the club," I said, glancing at the time. It was unlikely that anyone would be there yet, but I would give it a shot. I put Darling on speaker and pulled a hooded sweatshirt over my tank top and reached for my leather jacket and boots.

Darling reeled off the name of the place.

In the kitchen, I grabbed my coffee and poured it into a to-go cup.

"I'm heading over there now."

"I'll call you," she said and hung up.

A feeling of deep dread spread over me.

I'd met Clara. She wasn't the type just to disappear. She wasn't the type to hop a flight somewhere on a whim. Was she?

I texted Darling. "Have you called James?"

She wrote back. "Police said she's not officially missing yet. She's an adult."

"I'll call him," I said.

As the valet pulled my Maserati around to the front of the hotel, I dialed James's cell.

James was one of the great loves of my life. Many many years ago, when we were a couple, he'd received death threats for trying to expose corrupt cops in the San Francisco police department. Then, one of his own brothers in blue had shot and paralyzed him, condemning him to a wheelchair for the rest of his life.

We'd tried to make it work and ended up friends. But he would always own a small piece of my heart. We'd tried rekindling our love again after his beloved wife, Genevieve, died of breast cancer, but we were destined to only be friends. We were ill-fated lovers: He was a man of the law. I was a killer.

When James had been shot and paralyzed the doctors had questioned whether he'd ever be able to have children or even walk again, but he had Janie. His daughter was now in college.

My call went to voicemail. I left a message explaining what was going on and asked him to call me asap.

I texted Darling again.

"Any chance they went out of town? A road trip? An airplane trip?"

She immediately texted back.

"No. She would've answered her phone or text. She's a good girl. She knows her mama would worry. They were supposed to have lunch today. She'd never make her mother worry."

Dread spiked through me once again.

This was not good.

Then I was in my car, heading to the club. It was down by the water near the baseball stadium.

When I pulled up, the side door was open, and a delivery truck was parked next to it. A man was hauling cases of booze inside

I parked a little ways down the alley. Before getting out of the Maserati, I unlocked the glove box and took out my gun. I stuck it in my back waistband and got out.

I waited until the driver had climbed in the back of the truck, then I ran for the open back door.

I wandered through the back rooms and kitchen until I saw a light on.

A man sitting at a desk looking at a stack of papers jumped a foot out of his chair when I walked in. He was reaching for a gun and swearing when I held up my hands above my head.

"Jesus H Christ. You can't sneak up on a guy that way."

He lowered the gun to the desk.

"You're lucky I didn't squeeze one off," he said. "I been robbed before."

He was a heavyset man with a receding hairline and a shock of longish gray hair that stuck up from the middle of his head like a crown.

I was relieved to see a table off to one side that had six monitors showing live footage inside the club and out.

"I'm Gia Santella," I said. "I need your help."

He frowned.

"My friends were here last night, and they never made it home. I need to see your video footage from last night." I jutted my chin toward the security screens.

"You a cop?"

I shook my head. "No, I told you I'm a friend."

"You got a warrant?"

"That's why I'm here. It will take too long to get a warrant.

I'm hoping if something bad happened, say some creep kidnapped her or took her home with him—that I can find her sooner rather than later, know what I mean?"

He scowled. "I can't just let you waltz in and look at the footage."

"Why not?" I asked and folded my arms across my chest.

"It's weird."

"Yeah, this girl not answering her mama's calls is weird. That's why I'm here."

He shook his head. "I don't need any bad publicity. Something like this gets out, and girls are afraid to come here."

I was done playing nice.

"Maybe they *should* be afraid to come here if they never make it home."

He reached for his gun again, but before he could lift it, I had my own gun pointed at him.

"Easy now."

"It's time for you to leave," he said, keeping his hand on the desk but not moving it toward the gun anymore.

"You either show me the footage willingly, or I'll shoot you or knock you out or lock you up and look at it myself."

"All I have to do is yell and Felix, my delivery guy, will come running in."

I'd already heard the back door close loudly a few minutes before, so I shrugged.

"Do it, then."

He looked over at the bank of security screens. One camera showed the alley. The delivery truck was gone. He sighed and reached for a keyboard.

"Give me a sec to pull it up."

4

It took three hours for me to find the right footage.

The manager, resigned to his fate, poured us both some black sludge coffee from the maker on the desk, and we settled in to scan.

Finally, there was a very brief shot of Clara walking up to the front door of the club with two men and another woman. Presumably, the friends that Darling had mentioned.

Then they were inside, and I switched to watching footage from interior cameras.

The footage from inside the club was dark, and it was nearly impossible to distinguish one person from another in the flashing strobe lights on the dance floor. Booths lined the dance floor.

Most of the cameras showed wriggling masses of bodies that melded into one revolving blob in the dark.

Then I had the manager back everything up and begin again after Clara came in, keeping an eye on the footage showing the hallways leading to the bathroom.

Payoff.

At one point, I saw Clara and her girlfriend enter the hall

and then the bathroom. Nobody followed them. They left the bathroom and went down the empty hall without any other interactions.

I fast-forwarded the footage until the club closed at two. The cameras inside the club showed a mass exodus of people, again nearly impossible to tell one from the other.

I kept focused on the people emerging from the door of the club into the night in a steady stream. Then I spotted Clara with her three friends. They were a few feet away from the door when a man walked up behind her and touched her sleeve.

"Pause it here," I said.

The manager did.

"Can you blow it up?"

He shook his head.

I took a picture of the guy. It was a blurry, grainy photo. It showed the back of a guy's head. He wore a beanie. Longish hair hung out the back of it. There was something shiny—a ring on the hand touching Clara's sleeve. He wore a bulky hoodie. It was hard to tell if he was thin or built. His build was hidden by the sweatshirt, but his legs seemed thinner. He wore white sneakers. His feet were smallish.

I stared harder.

If I had to guess, I'd say the guy was just about six feet tall. His skin was darker than Clara's.

He looked like all the other guys leaving the club.

"Okay. Press play again."

The footage showed Clara turning to see the guy who had touched her arm. She was not smiling anymore. Words were exchanged. The man stopped, and she caught up with her group who hadn't turned around at all. Then they were off camera.

I watched to see what the man in the hoodie did. After a few seconds, he began walking in the direction Clara had gone.

"Okay, let's back it up," I said.

After another hour, I was able to find footage of the man entering the club. Again, it was from the back. The same hoodie. The same shoes. The same glinting ring on his right hand. But I couldn't see his face. He came alone.

"Do you know who that is? Is he a regular?"

The manager squinted. "Doesn't look familiar."

I stood and stretched. "When we saw her leaving, she was heading north. Which way would she have been going to get to her vehicle?"

"There's a lot in that direction. A pay lot. Otherwise there's no place else to park."

I tucked my gun in my back waistband and walked out without answering.

From the front door of the club, I saw the lot the club owner was talking about and headed over to it. It was half a block down from the club. It would probably fit fifty cars. I scanned it, then walked through it, staring at the ground. I wasn't sure what I was looking for. Maybe a button that had popped off a shirt or some other sign of a struggle. There was some trash but nothing else that could mean anything.

Fuck.

I had some blurry photos of some guy who spoke to Clara when she left the club and that was it.

I got back in my car and immediately texted the photos I'd taken of the footage of the guy. Then I dialed James's personal cell again. He picked up immediately.

"Gia! I just saw you called. Haven't listened to your message yet. Wait. Just got your text. Who is this dude?"

I filled him in and then included what I'd seen on the video footage at the club.

"Huh," he said. "That's not much is it?"

"Nope."

"I'll send someone to question the bartenders and doormen to see if they know who he is," he said. "Mind telling me how you got the manager to show you the footage without a warrant?"

"Don't ask, don't tell." I said and watched the club grow smaller in my rearview mirror.

"Damn it, Gia."

I didn't answer. I had a feeling he was secretly pleased I'd circumvented the red tape he would have to go through.

"The photo is shit," he finally said.

"Yeah, I know."

"Not sure we'd be able to get anything much better though. I'll have our experts look at it, but I think we're stuck with a shit picture. I can't imagine that shithole club has a high-tech surveillance system."

"Truth."

"I'll do some asking around."

"Thanks, James."

"You okay, Gia?"

"Same old shit."

"Rose is going to be fine."

James had always been like an uncle to her. She'd spent some time with him when she was here. Those were some of the only times she left the hotel room on her own.

"I know," I said. "I just miss her."

"And? I mean, Anthony seems like a good guy."

"He's fine. I mean besides the fact that his life is now mostly across the country, it's not bad."

"Gia, he's crazy about you."

"How do you know?" I said and laughed.

"I have my ways."

"Whatever," I said and scoffed.

"You seem pretty worried about this girl?"

"I am," I said. "Clara isn't the sort of girl to stand her mother up for lunch. Something is wrong. Very wrong."

5

As soon as I hung up with James, I dialed Darling.

"We're just sick over here," she said. "Clara obviously never came home. Her apartment is untouched. Her neighbor said her cat was mewling so loudly this morning it woke her."

"Damn."

"Mmmhmm."

"Who did she go out with? I saw some camera footage from the club. Another girl and two guys were with her?" Was one of them her boyfriend?"

"No. Her mama said they were fighting. That's why she left last night. She went to his house, got in an argument and then called her friends."

"What's Clara's boyfriend's name? Has anyone talked to him."

"He's here now. He's in the corner crying like a baby. He said she Snapchatted him at one and said she loved him. The picture was from the club. It had all four of them in the photo."

"Can you send it to me?"

"Honey, you obviously don't know how Snap works do you?"

I frowned. "And you do?"

"Uh, yeah. Unless you screenshot it, the picture disappears."

"I knew that."

"Mmmhmm."

"You think her boyfriend is telling the truth?"

"What are you getting at, Gia?"

I closed my eyes and exhaled. Their minds obviously hadn't gone to the dark place mine had.

"You're the one who said Clara was smart about everything except boys."

"I don't like him because he wants to get married and have kids like yesterday," she said. "He loves her, but that girl is going to change the world. She's not allowed to get married and have kids until she's forty at the earliest."

I laughed. "Is there anything else you don't like about him?"

At first I couldn't hear her because she was whispering.

"Huh?" I said and she answered louder in a stage whisper:

"He. Smokes. Pot."

I laughed again.

"Uh, okay," I said. "What was he doing last night after Clara left?"

"After the fight, he and his roommate stayed up talking and playing video games. They both got drunk and fell asleep in the living room with Alien playing in the background on the TV. Alisha's sister woke them when she came knocking."

"Okay. So, in the footage from the club, some guy touched Clara's arm on the way out. I tried to get a screenshot, but the quality is shit. I sent it to James to see if they can do some magic with it. James is going to send some detectives to question the bouncer and bartender when the club opens up again later this afternoon."

"Tell him thank you," Darling said in a subdued voice.

"What else can I do?"

"I just don't know, Gia." She sounded exhausted.

"What are you guys doing now?"

"We're all heading to church. Going to start a prayer chain."

I sat there for a second and then said, "Oh."

I had parted ways with religion a long time ago. My mother had been a believer, but I didn't know how I could believe in a God who allowed everyone I loved to be murdered.

"You could join us," Darling said in a soft voice.

I didn't know why, but her words made a sob rise in my throat.

"I'm good."

I hung up.

I was parked in front of my hotel, and only when I hung up did I notice the tizzy I'd sent the valet parkers in. They were running over and then after seeing me on the phone, backing off. Now they were conferencing at the valet podium.

Dang. Were they afraid of me because I was the owner? I felt awful.

Finally one of them glanced over at me. I smiled and crooked a finger.

He ran over and opened my door.

"Miss Santella?"

"Hi, Nolan," I said, reading his name tag.

"Welcome home."

"Thank you," I said. "I have a favor to ask you."

"Anything, Miss Santella."

"Could you keep my vehicle parked up front here in the circle drive in case I need to leave again right away?"

"Of course."

"Thank you."

I handed him a crisp one hundred dollar bill.

I didn't want the valet parkers to ever be afraid to come up to my vehicle again. I wanted them to race to see who could get there first.

Nolan had just stepped inside the vehicle, when I spoke.

"I heard you placed in the Vans Triple Crown on the North Shore last month."

His mouth dropped open. "Yeah. Yeah. It was pretty cool."

"Congratulations. That's nothing to sneeze at. That's a tough tournament."

He nodded.

"When's your next tournament?"

"Um, in two weeks. It's in Santa Barbara."

"Santa Barbara, California, or Santa Barbara in the Azores."

"The Azores."

"Wow. I've always wanted to go there. I used to live in Barcelona but never made it," I said. "Before you go, talk to Carlisle. He knows the owner of the Ritz-Carlton there. We'd like to comp you a few rooms while you are there."

"Thanks, Miss Santella."

I walked into the lobby.

I had made a point to know the name of every single employee in the hotel and a little bit about what was going on in their lives. The hotel manager sent me profiles with pictures attached.

If I was going to own a fucking hotel, I was going to make it the best damn hotel in San Francisco.

I would make every guest feel like a rock star.

And that started with making my staff feel a sense of ownership.

I wanted them to feel like we were a family.

It would take time, but it would happen.

Anybody who didn't feel that way would be paid to move on.

I'd just gotten into my room and kicked off my boots when the phone rang.

At first I couldn't make out what was being said, but then I realized it was Darling.

She was weeping.

I closed my eyes and shook my head.

I didn't want her to say it.

"They found them."

"Oh, Darling," I said, my heart breaking for her and her friend.

"All of them dead."

"What?"

They must have died in a terrible car crash, was all I could think.

But then Darling's voice grew clearer.

"The car was in a field between Benicia and the small town of Cordelia where the I-80 freeway meets I-680 on the way to Sacramento."

"What happened?"

More sobbing.

"They was executed. All four shot in the head."

I was stunned. I shook my head, at a loss for words.

The image of Clara and her four friends assassinated and left in a cornfield filled me with horror and fury.

"I'm so sorry," I said, but I was thinking, *What the fuck kind of monster would kill that sweet girl and her friends?*

"The cops said maybe it was a drug deal gone bad."

"What? Are you kidding me?"

"It's because they're black, Gia. It's because they are black."

Rage filled me. I could feel it race through my body until my fists were curled and clenched.

"Clara never touched a drug in her life," Darling said. "She has MS. She knows if she does drugs it could kill her. She never would do it. Her cousin overdosed when she was in high school. She would never, ever do drugs."

I nodded even though Darling couldn't see me.

"I believe you," I said and then very, very carefully asked my next question. "What about her friends?"

"Nope. They're all college kids. All drink and have fun, but no drugs. Not a one of them. I had them all to my house lots of times."

"You're sure?"

Kids lied to the adults in their lives.

"Gia, I'm damn sure. And I'm also damn sure about something else–the cops are going to say it's a drug deal gone bad because those four kids are black. You understand? They are going to write off some cold-blooded murders and blame it on the victims."

Darling's voice was now filled with the same rage I felt.

I heard a woman wailing in the background. And heard people trying to comfort her.

It was a horrific sound.

Maybe the worst sound I'd ever heard.

"They won't even try as hard to find who did this if they think it's a drug deal gone bad. You and me both know that. All I want is justice. Her mama just wants to know who could do this to her baby. Who could do this? What kind of evil person could take this baby girl away from us? The cops don't care. They aren't even going to try. The killer is going to get away with it. Mark my words."

"Darling," I finally said. "I'm not going to let that happen. I'm going to find whoever did this, and I'm going to make them pay."

6

JAMES CALLED RIGHT AFTER I HUNG UP.

I was in the bathroom trying to brush my teeth. I spit out the toothpaste and answered the phone.

"I heard," I said in a dull voice before he could speak.

"I'm going to go out there," he said. "Want to hitch a ride? I'm about five out from you."

"I'll be waiting."

I hung up.

The last thing I wanted to do was see that beautiful girl's dead body.

But it might help. It might not. But it just might.

It wouldn't be pretty. But I needed to see for myself. Maybe there was something at the scene that would give me a clue who did this.

Back in my living room, I pulled my boots back on, grabbed my motorcycle jacket and headed down to the hotel lobby.

James pulled up in the standard-issue FBI ride—black Crown Victoria. Except his vehicle was specially equipped for someone who didn't have use of their legs. He'd only been with the FBI for a month now. He'd finally let his unreasonable allegiance to the San Francisco Police Department go. I hopped in, giving him a wry smile. He nodded at a hot coffee with steam coming off it in the cup holder. He was holding the same thing in one hand.

"Thanks."

James was still good looking, damn it. He looked like the Black Ken Doll. Fit body. Cheekbones for days. His dark skin didn't have a single wrinkle that I could find, and I was giving him a good once over.

"What?"

"You still look as good as the day I met you."

He laughed.

"I think you look even better than the day I met you, Gia."

I grinned. "No wonder I like hanging out with you."

Then he grew serious.

"You sure you're good to see the scene?" he asked.

"Who am I going to be?"

"Huh?"

"What am I? Your assistant? Your note taker. Why would they let me crawl all over a quadruple homicide scene?"

"I'm a Fed. I don't have to explain shit."

"Nice to see you owning the power of the new job," I said. "What have you heard?"

"Not much. A farmer found the car parked in the middle of his field, and when he got close, saw the blood and hightailed it out of there to call 911."

"What time?"

"Four in the morning. It was still dark."

"How many people have trampled the scene?"

James grinned.

"The detective is an old buddy of mine from the city."

"Aha," I said. "That explains why they are letting you on the scene."

Unless something was under the jurisdiction of the FBI or there was an agreement to work a case together, local cops were hesitant to mix with federal cops and vice versa.

"He knows you're coming?"

James nodded. "I told him it was personal, and he said to come on by. He's a good guy. Name's Hicks. He never wanted to move up in ranks. He's still hoofing it on the homicide squad, and he's a stickler for maintaining a scene. The coroner would've already been there, but with the budget cuts, they only have one deputy on duty, and she was tied up in a four-car crash until just a bit ago."

I nodded.

This was good.

It would be a pretty clean scene. Not that I was a detective and would know what to look for, but I really wanted to get there and see it as the killer left it.

Riding along with James was ideal.

It meant unfettered access.

But something was bothering me.

"This Hicks, when's the last time you spoke to him?"

"Been about five years. We sort of lost touch, but we're brothers in blue, Gia. We have each other's back for life."

I decided not to point out that the reason he was paralyzed was from those so-called brothers in blue who'd turned on him.

"Let me be blunt, then," I said. "Is he racist?"

James gave me the side-eye. "Um, have we met? Gia, I'm black. If he was racist, do you think I would say he's a good guy?"

"How can I put this?" I began. "Does he assume that any black person who is murdered might have done something to cause it?"

James actually pulled over to the side of the road. We were just about to get on the Bay Bridge. He turned to face me.

"What?"

I told him what Darling had said.

"The cops who did the death notification said something about a drug deal gone bad."

"Jeeesus," James said. He reached for his phone without saying a word, keeping his eyes on me.

"You might want to know what the cops who did the notification said," he began. "They said it was a drug deal gone bad."

I heard another voice coming from the phone but couldn't understand anything. James nodded, keeping his eyes trained on me.

He mumbled things like, "okay" and "I see" and "oh boy."

Then he hung up.

"What?"

"They found a big bag of weed in the vehicle."

"How big is big?"

"Dealer quantity."

Fuck.

"I know Darling's girl might be clean, but can she vouch for the other three?" James asked.

I just shook my head.

"It doesn't make sense," I said. "If it was a drug deal gone bad, why would they leave a bag of weed there?"

James nodded and started up his vehicle. "It's a little sketchy."

"A little?" I said, raising my voice.

He shrugged.

"I hope your detective buddy does the right thing and investigates this the way it needs to be investigated, because if he doesn't make the killer pay, I will."

James shook his head.

"I. Did. Not. Hear. You. Say. That."

"Whatever," I said and reached over to turn up the radio.

7

THE CAR WAS IN THE MIDDLE OF A FIELD JUST NORTH OF BENICIA.
Because the hills were slightly rolling, only the top of the vehicle could be seen from the highway. We pulled off the highway and parked behind half a dozen other cars pulled off on the shoulder—a few squads, a few unmarked, and the morgue's paddy wagon—an extra-long, unmarked blue van without windows.

"We walking in?" I said to James.

He squinted toward the field. "Looks like it."

He was reaching back for his wheelchair when I got it out for him. Before I could offer any more help, he'd hopped into it and was in front of the car, heading for the field.

I eyed the rough terrain, big clumps of dirt, and corn stalks, but James made a beeline and was already in the field by the time the cop parked at the front of the line of cars noticed us.

He was a community service officer—an unarmed volunteer. In this case, a twenty-something chubby kid with a cowlick and freckles. He was sort of jogging toward us with a concerned look on his face. He obviously wasn't doing a good job guarding the crime scene since we were already in the field. He started to shout when James held up his FBI badge.

The kid slowed his pace and nodded, but gave me a look.

I had to admit I didn't look like FBI.

We were about the furthest thing from a Fox Mulder and Dana Skully team you could imagine.

James in his wheelchair, me in my beat-up black motorcycle jacket and hair that was so messy it was bordering on dreads. I tried running my fingers through it in the car and then finally gave up. I had swiped on some pink lipstick during the drive, but it was an obviously half-assed effort to look put-together.

I could've at least pretended to look like Dana Skully from the *X-Files* and wore my black Armani suit and a cute trench coat with low heels and a cross necklace. I did have clothes like that, but nope, for some reason I'd thought it'd be a good idea to wear the scrungy clothes I already was wearing.

I looked like some unteethbrushed, wearing-the-same-clothes-she-wore-the-day-before rocker chick who had been up all night drinking too much at a party and managed to convince the detective she seduced into her bed to let her tag along on a homicide investigation.

I had to give it to James—he didn't give a flying fuck what anyone thought.

All my thoughts in this direction came to an abrupt halt when the reality of what we were walking up to hit me.

James had been navigating the ruts in the fields handily when he came to a stop, and I almost crashed into the back of his wheelchair.

Before us was an area marked off by crime scene tape.

Three people with black jackets that said "Coroner" on the back in yellow were in various stages of tending to the four bodies that had been laid out on the trampled stalks of corn.

The bodies were covered with white sheets. I swallowed,

trying to get rid of the feeling that something was stuck in my throat. That poor girl. A coroner was working near her feet, tucking them into the black body bag she was lying on top of. As he moved her, her head lolled, and I saw her eyes were wide open.

James followed my gaze.

"You want to do the ID? Maybe spare the family from having to come down to the morgue."

"Yes." I said without hesitation. I would do anything I could to spare that family more pain and suffering.

"How sure are you?"

"One hundred percent. I recognize the birthmark on her left cheek too."

"Wait here," he said and headed toward another man nearby.

This man was dressed in faded jeans and a thick flannel shirt. He had on a John Deere tractor ball cap, and every few minutes, he would lean his head outside the crime scene tape and spit tobacco juice onto the ground.

His face lit up in a smile when he saw James, and he pumped James's hand heartily.

Must be Hicks.

James said something, and the man glanced over at me and nodded.

I gave a solemn nod back.

He didn't look like a detective. He looked like an old dude ready to go grab a coffee and donut with his cronies and play cribbage.

I suddenly felt much better about my outfit choices that day.

As I waited, another police SUV arrived, navigating the field's ruts and hollows and then pulled up. Hicks directed it to park right in front of where the bodies were, effectively blocking my view and that of the other cops standing around beside me.

After a few minutes of conversation, James came back.

"We're good to go. Hicks is going to have you do the positive ID as soon as the coroner has a few seconds. These are the deputy coroners just bagging and tagging. The head forensic pathologist is still over at the car. She'll be over soon."

8

Suddenly, I was freezing. I wrapped my arms around my chest and realized I was shivering.

James was over talking to some cops, and I stood there alone feeling sorry for myself. I didn't want to see Clara dead again.

I pulled out my phone and dialed Darling.

"Oh, Gia," she said in a defeated voice.

"I'm going to do the ID for the family, if that's okay with you. They said I could."

It was quiet for a few seconds, and then she said in a small voice, "Thank you."

"How are you holding up?"

"About as well as can be expected. Trying to stay strong for Alisha."

"You're a queen."

A stifled laugh.

"I feel like an old woman today for the first time in my life," she said.

"You'll never be an old woman, Darling," I said, watching James walk over and talk to a woman dressed in a white lab coat.

They both looked over at me and then James nodded. "I'll call you when we're done here."

I hung up before Darling answered and took a deep breath before walking over to where James and the woman stood.

When I was in front of them, James introduced me to the forensic pathologist.

"Gia, this is Patricia Cargill."

She had spiky blonde hair, ice blue eyes, and a strong jawline. She looked like she knew she could kick my ass if she wanted to. I rarely met another woman who gave me that vibe. She shook my hand and then lit a cigarette, offering me one. I didn't look at James as I accepted one from her pack.

"I only smoke out at scenes," she said.

"Aren't you worried about contaminating them?" I asked.

She gave me a derisive look.

"Or not..." I said lightly, accepting the light she offered me from a cheap orange plastic lighter.

"You ready for this?"

I nodded.

She led me around the police SUV. Behind it were four bodies. She led me to the smallest one.

Then she crouched down beside the head. I did so too.

She inhaled her cigarette and gave me a look. I nodded. She reached over and plucked a rock that was holding the sheet down to the ground and then lifted it.

Clara's green eyes were dull and lifeless. The first thing I did was reach for her eyelids to close her eyes. The pathologist didn't stop me. I saw the small beauty mark on her left cheek. I tried to ignore the gaping hole just above her right eye.

She'd been executed, point blank.

"It's Clara."

Before I could react, the pathologist had pulled the sheet back over her face and stood.

I took a little longer to stand up beside her.

"Does she have defensive wounds?" I asked.

She searched my eyes for a long few seconds and then shook her head.

She took a drag off the cigarette and exhaled before speaking.

"This is all part of the homicide investigation, so keep it to yourself, but there's nothing like that. Nothing under her nails. No defensive wounds. It's as if someone just walked up to her and shot her without her realizing it until it was over."

The woman gave a barely perceptible nod.

"What about the others?"

"The other girl *does* have defensive wounds, leading me to think she was shot last. The other two were shot in the back of the head, not the front."

"Were they killed in the SUV?"

That garnered me a curious look.

"No. Bodies were put there after it was driven out here."

"Huh," I said.

"Yeah."

"So this isn't the murder scene?"

"Nope. That's why so many people are trampling it. We don't know where they were killed. But from the way they died, I would suspect the four of them weren't standing together. Otherwise, at least three of them would have defensive wounds, not just one of them."

"The killer picked them off one by one," I said.

"Might be."

We walked back over to James.

"Anything else you want to see here?" he said.

"I don't think so."

"Want to meet Hicks?"

I eyed the man in the flannel shirt. Yeah. I wanted to meet

him. I wanted to see if I could tell if he was going to write off these murders as a drug deal gone bad because the victims were black. Of course, meeting him wouldn't tell me this. Or maybe it would.

The man hitched up his jeans and headed over when James gave a low whistle.

"Nice to meet you, Miss Santella."

"Thanks for allowing me to come out. It means a lot to the family."

"You might have heard that we don't think the actual murders took place here, so that was an easy call. We've got some crime scene stuff to do here, but really we don't have a hell of a lot. We need to find that murder scene."

"James speaks highly of you," I said.

The man laughed. "We do go back a ways. Way before those corrupt bastards took over and turned against us good cops. They'll never pay enough for what they did to James."

My respect for the man instantly doubled. I nodded.

"I'm a little concerned these deaths will be written off as a drug deal gone bad," I said and watched the man's reaction.

He scowled. "I'm not going to lie. I'm getting some pressure from above to lean that way. And it's going to be an uphill battle to convince them to look elsewhere since we found cocaine splattered all over their bodies as if there was a struggle and a baggie broke. And then there was that bag of marijuana."

"Fuck."

He didn't flinch. "I'm just being straight up with you."

"That girl? The one I identified? She's studying law, working as a paralegal, spends her spare time volunteering at a dog shelter, and was the fucking valedictorian of her high school graduating class."

He nodded.

"Just so you know," I added.

I turned to James. "Let's go."

"Nice to meet you, Miss Santella," he said again.

"Likewise," I said and then paused. "I'm counting on you to not let them sweep this under the rug."

He took off his ball cap and ran his fingers through some messy hair.

"That's a tall order," he said. "Especially for someone so close to retirement and life on a beach somewhere with a cold beer."

"I'm sure you can handle it."

9

We were pretty quiet on the drive back.

At one point, James said, "Do you feel better after meeting Hicks? That he won't write this one off?"

I answered honestly. "I'm not sure. I mean I've known him for, like, five minutes."

"Fair enough."

"Thanks for letting me go out there."

James tapped the steering wheel and gave a long sigh, keeping his eyes on the road as we entered the Benicia Bridge. "I worry I gave you fuel for your fire."

I shifted in my seat to face him.

"Seriously? You knew I was going after this the second I called. Nothing has changed."

"I know. I just think for once in your life, you should let law enforcement do its job."

"Oh fuck off. You know why I feel the way I do about 'law enforcement doing its job,' James. Come off it."

He laughed and then grew quiet.

I reached over and touched his arm.

"It's sweet that you still care, though."

"Now, you fuck off," he said.

Traffic slowed and he quickly glanced over at me. We exchanged a look that made me swallow hard. I would always love this man, and I knew he would always love me. But we would never be together like that.

For some reason it was comforting to realize that our love would never be realized again but also would never die.

Then his attention was on the road as angry drivers honked at someone driving too slow on the bridge.

"I know you don't know the other kids, but can you think of any reason why someone would want Clara dead?" he asked.

I couldn't. And told him so.

He dropped me off at the hotel, and I immediately headed toward my car. I was going straight to the house where Clara's family was gathered. Darling had texted me an address on the drive back.

I pulled up to a house in a neighborhood in San Bruno, south of San Francisco.

Cars were lined up on both sides of the road.

When I reached the porch, a woman with red, swollen eyes opened the door for me. She had a phone propped between her ear and shoulder. She gestured to me as she continued talking.

"We don't know yet," she said. "It's going to be at First Baptist in Hayward. Yes."

She met my eyes and pointed. I walked the way she pointed and was soon in a great room full of people. The great room had an open kitchen area with a dining room that opened up into a large living room with several couches, chairs, and a fireplace. Little kids were running around, and teenagers were herding them toward another room. Every chair was filled. The room was full of conversation. A few people were even laughing. I stood there uncertainly until I found Darling in the crowd. She was seated at one end of a dining room table, reigning over it in her queenly manner.

She crooked a finger with an obscenely long pink and gold painted fingernail at me. I obeyed and wove through the darting kids towards her.

Of course I did.

I leaned down and kissed her cheek.

That's when I saw Clara's mom, Alisha Parks, at her elbow. She stood up and gave me a tight hug.

"Thank you. Thank you so much for going to see Clara for us."

I nodded, dry mouthed and at a loss for words.

A young woman had grabbed a folding chair and set it between Darling and Clara's mother.

I sat down gratefully.

"We were just about to pray," Mrs. Parks said. And then we all held hands.

A woman at the other end of the table stood, keeping hold of the hands on either side of her and the room grew quiet. Then she spoke in a silky but authoritative voice.

"Dear Lord Jesus, we thank you for your presence here with us today. We thank you, oh God, for your angels and saints welcoming our sister Clara up into your arms today, dear Lord."

"Amen," several women said.

"We believe in your righteousness, oh Lord, and while we don't understand your ways, we trust that whatever you do is the right thing, oh God.

More people chimed in with affirmations and "amens."

"While our hearts are breaking right now for the loss of Clara, we know, we know for a fact, dear Lord, she is with you now in all your eternal glory. We know she is in your hands and that she is laughing and happy."

More "amens."

"And Lord, we just pray for the person or persons who took her life. May you bless them. May you lead them to do the right thing and seek your forgiveness, dear Lord.

My eyes popped open, along with my mouth. I looked over at Darling. Her eyes were still closed, and she was nodding.

What the fuck.

I squeezed Darling's hand. She opened her eyes, and I made a face showing my incredulousness.

They were talking about forgiveness for a cold-blooded killer who had just taken a beautiful soul and destroyed a family?

Darling peeked through her long eyelashes and gave me a warning shake of her head.

I nearly ripped my hand out of hers, but she clenched my hand tighter, her long-ass nails digging into my palm.

Jesus.

The woman continued praying.

Finally, the prayer was over. I tried not to rip my hands away from Darling and Clara's mother's grip.

What the fuckity fuck?

Clara's mother was smiling at me.

"Gia, you seem surprised."

I didn't know what to say, but it didn't matter because she continued.

"We are God-fearing people. We don't believe in vengeance. We believe in forgiveness and love."

"Okay," I said. "I get that. But to pray for—"

"My daughter's murderer?" she interrupted.

"Yes!"

"We forgive him; not for his sake, but for ours."

"I guess I don't get that," I said.

She smiled again.

"That doesn't mean we don't believe in justice. I also pray

that he is arrested and serves time for what he has done. But more than that, I pray that he asks God for forgiveness."

I shook my head. "Don't you want him to pay? To pay for what he did?"

She nodded. "That's why we are hoping there is an arrest. Yes."

"I want him dead."

Her eyes widened. "I do not. My heart is broken. My life will never be the same again, but another death will not help me. His death will not bring back Clara."

I exhaled and nodded, not trusting myself to speak.

"Come on, Gia," Darling said and stood. "Let's go take a walk."

"Is there anything I can do to help?" I asked Mrs. Parks.

She smiled tightly. "Just pray for us."

I smiled back. I wasn't going to promise something I couldn't do.

Darling led me out to the front room.

"Gia, the best thing you can do is let the police handle this."

"That's not what you said this morning."

"I know. I know. But your brand of justice is not what Alisha wants or needs right now."

"Fine. But I'm still going to try to find the killer. I just don't trust the cops on this one."

"This God-fearing family has already forgiven the killer."

"That's whack. You know it. And I know it." I was pissed.

"Mmmhmm," she said in that maddening noncommittal way she had. "You can help but I don't want you to do what you would normally do."

I put my hands on my waist. "Oh yeah, and what's that?"

"You know, your swimming-with-the-fishes stuff."

If I hadn't been so pissed, I would have burst into laughter.

"You stereotyping me?"

"Oh hush now."

"What are you trying to say, Darling? Spit it out."

"What I'm telling you is that you heard it yourself—they don't believe in an eye for an eye, Gia."

"Huh."

"Yeah. Huh. That's all you've got to say?"

"I'll find the killers and then decide."

"Gia!"

I walked out, leaving her there spluttering.

I would handle it my way.

Maybe I'd let the killer live. Maybe I wouldn't.

I wasn't making any promises.

But deep down inside, I knew I would let him live.

I couldn't go against that grieving mother with the faith to move mountains.

10

By the time I got home, it was late. I showered, ordered a cheeseburger from room service and started binge watching the last season of *Game of Thrones*.

I fell asleep in front of the TV. When I woke, I thought of Clara's boyfriend getting drunk and falling asleep in front of the TV. Then I thought of something and, without looking at the time, dialed James.

As soon as he answered, I realized it was two in the morning. Oops.

"Clara's stepdad is a diplomat who just returned to the US."

I heard his wife in the background. "Who on earth is that, James?"

"Gia," he said.

"Oh, tell her hello," she said.

"I'll check into that first thing in the morning," James said and hung up.

Damn.

That morning, I called Darling.

"You still in town?" I asked.

"I'm staying at my place in the city for now. Helping Alisha all I can."

"You're a good woman."

"Hey, didn't Mrs. Parks say Clara's dad was a diplomat?"

Darling paused for a second. "Clara's stepdad. Alisha remarried. Jackson is her stepdad. They get along fine."

Suddenly Darling sobbed. "I mean they got along fine."

"I'm so sorry."

"Her daddy owns a chain of coffee shops in the South Bay and a small roasting company in Brazil where he gets his beans. Why?"

"What about the stepdad?" I ask. "Can you think of anyone he had dealings with as a diplomat that might want to harm Clara?"

"I'll ask Alisha when I get a chance."

"Thanks."

"I have to go. We're heading over to the funeral home to make arrangements. I just wrote the eulogy."

"Oh, Darling. I'm so sorry."

"Yeah. My heart is broken, Gia. Just shattered."

I hadn't seen her so down since her husband died of a heart attack a few years back.

"I'm going to find out who did this, Darling."

"You know how Alisha feels. I don't have to remind you, do I?"

"Nope."

I hung up.

As much as I wanted to hunt down the killer, I was at a loss as to what to do next.

Then I made the mistake of checking my hotel email account and spent the next three hours handling hotel business.

I was taken out of that world when James called.

"We made an arrest."

"*What?*" I was genuinely surprised. There hadn't been any strong leads, or I would've been all over them.

"Dude walked into the station and turned himself in."

"You're fucking kidding?"

"Said he figured he was gonna get caught anyway so wanted to confess. Said the kids wanted to buy drugs, so he had them meet him in the field, and he shot one when they pulled something out of their pocket. It ended up being a phone. He said he panicked and shot the others."

Bullshit.

"Does that jive with what they found at the crime scene?" I asked.

"Not at all."

"Give me his name."

James didn't argue. "Robert Enzenauer."

I opened my laptop. I used my meager hacking skills to look him up.

When I didn't find anything, I called my pal Danny, a world-class hacker.

"This the guy who killed Clara?" he asked.

I swallowed.

"You knew her?"

"We met at Darling's place once."

His voice cracked.

"I'm sorry."

"Thanks," he said in a small voice.

"Yeah," I said. "This dude turned himself in, said he's good for it. Says it was a drug deal gone bad. He's waiving his rights too."

"That's fucking weird."

"Yeah, I know." I didn't mention another detail that made the dude's story implausible. That whole operation would require two people—someone to drive the car that was left in the field and someone to drive the getaway car.

"What do you think?" Danny asked.

"He's taking the fall for someone else. There is definitely someone else involved here."

"Any motive?"

"I can't think of any right now. I've been trying to for days. Maybe her diplomat stepdad pissed someone off?"

"Give me his name."

I did.

"Let me see what I can find on both of them."

"Thanks, Danny."

I set my alarm for eight the next morning. I was going to get up, get ready, and see if I could visit the supposed killer in jail.

I showered and regretted the espresso I'd had at eleven p.m. My mind was buzzing.

When I finally crawled into bed it was close to three in the morning—the witching hour.

I lay there, wide awake, mulling over the events of the past week.

I tossed and turned, trying to make what I'd seen and heard make sense.

But it never did.

Then it struck me.

This family, full of love and forgiveness, was the polar opposite of me.

I lived for vendetta. I believe in an eye-for-an-eye.

They forgave the killer before they knew who it was or what sick motive he or she might have had.

They were about peace.

I was about violence.

They believed in forgiveness.

I believed in exacting justice with a vengeance.

Maybe if my life had turned out differently I would be able to understand them better.

If I hadn't been raped. If my parents hadn't been murdered.

If so many people I loved hadn't died terrible, violent deaths, maybe I could try to see from their perspective.

But as hard as I tried, I just couldn't understand their forgiveness.

And because I couldn't, I felt a hole inside. Something inside me was missing.

I loved deeply. But I didn't love like that.

That was beyond anything I had ever experienced.

I thought about it for hours. I wondered what it would be like to be the sort of person who could forgive a killer who'd assassinated their child? It was incomprehensible to me.

No matter how long my thoughts chewed at the scenario, looking at it from different angles and views, it made no sense to me.

Finally, close to dawn, I fell asleep.

11

A FEW HOURS LATER, I WAS UP AND DRESSED IN MY SOFTEST AND most-faded black jeans, motorcycle boots, a worn gray T-shirt, and my super thick leather motorcycle jacket. It was usually cold in the jail's visiting room.

Right before I left my hotel suite, I checked my phone.

Danny had sent me some information.

The stepdad didn't seem to have any dark secrets. At least not any obvious ones. I was glad. The last thing Alisha Parks needed was to find out her daughter was murdered because of something her husband did. That might send the woman even further off the deep end.

The killer was an ex-con who had served time for auto theft.

Danny couldn't find anything that hinted at a violent past.

In fact, for the past decade, he'd been a respectable citizen, managing a drive-thru oil change shop. He was married with an eight-year-old daughter.

Danny said there was something about the kid—some kind of disability or illness.

There had been a bankruptcy, and bills to a children's hospital had been included in the settlement.

Maybe having a sick kid and the stress of mounting bills had led him back to a life of crime.

But murder? Maybe. You play with fire you get burned.

He wouldn't be the first person who only wanted to either sell drugs or get high and then ended up with a murder rap.

If he hadn't set out to kill anyone, it would make more sense that he turned himself in.

I was really curious to see what he was like.

During my drive to the jail, Danny texted me again. Dude didn't have a big rap sheet, but his brother did. Very interesting. His brother had served time for manslaughter. He punched some guy outside a bar and killed him. Oops. There were a few other violent arrests and an assault with a deadly weapon. He'd only been paroled last year. Very fucking interesting.

The brother's name was Donald Enzenauer. I'd bet my last dollar he was the accomplice. It had taken two people driving two vehicles to leave the car out in the corn field.

Danny's text said besides his record, there was no trace of Donald Enzenauer anywhere.

The drive to the Fairfield jail from the city normally took thirty minutes, but shitty Bay Area traffic being what it was, it took me ninety excruciating minutes.

I'd gone through my entire female rapper playlist and was on to old-school Eminem when I finally saw the turnoff for the jail.

Once inside the lobby, I waited in line with a handful of other people. A young woman with a tattoo on her neck, a heavyset woman with a toddler racing around the lobby with a toy car, a sad-eyed older man in baggy pants, and a guy in a badly fitting suit.

When I got to the head of the line with my paperwork, I slid over my driver's license and the papers and then was told to go back and sit down and wait.

I watched as the older man in baggy pants was called and directed to step through the metal detector. The alarm went off, and he was told to empty his pockets and stick everything in one of the lockers. It was painstaking watching how slowly he did all of this, carefully laying out every item on the bench near the locker:

Pocket knife? Seriously, dude?

Lip balm.

Money clip with a thick wad of cash.

Black hair comb.

Handkerchief.

Thick and worn leather wallet.

A granola bar. (I'm not making this up.)

A pack of gum.

A cheap, plastic lighter. (Again—seriously, dude?)

A nail clipper. (He'd obviously never visited anyone in jail before.)

A small painted rock.

By this point, everyone in the lobby was transfixed, waiting to see what the guy was going to pull out of his pockets next. Even the toddler had paused his car noises to watch.

Finally, the old man was done and everything was securely locked up.

He was waved through the metal detectors and was on his merry way.

He probably weighed ten pounds lighter without his baggy pockets full of very important items.

Then it was my turn. I took off my leather jacket and handed it to the guard, knowing the metal would be an issue. He patted the jacket down and then waved me through the metal detectors. Of course, I passed with flying colors.

Then he pointed me to an elevator.

Second floor.

I shrugged my jacket back on, glad for the warmth again in the chilly building and headed toward the elevators.

The second floor contained three cubbies with glass separating me from another room where a man sat seated.

He had pale, pockmarked skin and a weak chin. His longish brown hair looked greasy and stuck to his head. He reminded me of a weasel. His eyes were the only things that didn't seem skittish about him. They took me in without blinking, examining me warily.

I picked up the phone. My hand was shaking.

This was the fucking piece of shit who killed Clara and her friends.

"I'm Gia Santella." My voice was ice. I hated this fucker's face and everything about him, but I had to play it cool.

"Why are you here?" he said.

"I think you're full of shit."

He scowled. "Bitch, you joking?"

"I'm not a bitch, asswipe. I've just got your number. You may have killed Clara and her friends, but there's more to your story. Way more."

He stood. His face had grown red.

"I don't have time for this bullshit."

"You got nothing but time now, pal."

He shook his head and hung up the phone. He walked over and knocked on a door, and a guard came and opened it, letting him into the next room out of my view.

I hung up the phone and stood.

Well that went well.

Fuck.

12

Back in my hotel suite, I took care of some hotel business on my computer. I'd lost track of time and was just about to order some food from room service when my phone rang.

Anthony.

I let it go to voicemail.

I was slightly miffed with him and being childish by not answering his call.

We didn't have a commitment. We were not exclusive. Far from it.

I mean, he knew I still would be with Ryder if I had a choice.

I'd picked Ryder over him once already.

But still.

I was miffed because there'd been a glossy spread of him in *People* magazine saying he was the year's hottest and most-eligible bachelor. Then there had been little bubbles of socialites and six pretty—and apparently single—women and little blurbs about what would make them a good match.

I'd been okay with that.

It was when I turned the page and saw him talking to each

and every one of those women in the six individual photo bubbles...

The images had been ranked from one to six in order of who was the best match.

It was girl number one that made me pause.

She had long, dark hair. Like me. She had huge black eyes with luscious lashes. Like me. And she had major curves in all the right places. Like me. She lived in San Francisco. Like me.

And she was a fucking millionaire. Like me.

She was a self-made millionaire. Unlike me.

(I'd had a head start with my inheritance. True, I'd tripled it on my own, but I'd been given a hand.) This woman had grown up poor in Brazil and had scratched and scraped her way up and built a fucking fashion and jewelry and cosmetics empire.

Her success—more than her beauty—was slightly intimidating.

I examined the photo of the two of them carefully. I didn't like what I saw.

He was leaning back, laughing, clearly comfortable as fuck in her company.

She had her head thrown back like she'd just had an orgasm, and I hated her for looking that sexy in front of Anthony.

The green-eyed beast overtook me. For one second.

I'd never been the jealous type and had no intention of becoming that way now.

I LISTENED TO THE VOICEMAIL.

"Gia! I just landed in the city. I must see you. I flew out here just to see you. I wanted to surprise you but then realized how stupid that was. Remember last time you were surprised by an out of town guest when we got to your place? So I'm calling first.

But I'm on my way over. I'll wait in the lobby until I hear from you."

I smiled.

I'd been out on a date with Anthony, and when we returned to my hotel room, we walked in to find Ryder sitting on my couch in nothing but a towel. Anthony left, and I'd spent the next week with Ryder. For some reason Anthony hadn't given up on me.

I had no reason to be jealous. I was the one he had called.

Not the super-hot cosmetics and jewelry queen.

I texted him back. "See you soon."

I stripped and hopped into a hot shower.

As I let the water run down my face, I allowed myself to feel the lust building in me for Anthony's visit. As I lathered the soap over my body, my skin and nerves felt electric.

He was coming over just in time.

I'd been horny for weeks. Being in the same car with James had amplified it. Despite all our fundamental relationship differences, we'd always had the hottest sex life around. Even after his accident.

I'd been about to resort to unsatisfying phone sex with Ryder.

Which was better than nothing. Actually, it was a lot better than going to find someone at a bar. Those days were long gone for me.

I shuddered, remembering how easy it had been to go home with a stranger—or worse, bring them home with me.

Even so, I smiled thinking about it.

Nothing bad had happened, and I'd had some pretty hot experiences.

Thinking of them now made me even hornier.

Anthony could not get there soon enough.

Finally, my phone rang.

"I'm in the lobby. I'm starving. Do you want to come down and grab a bite to eat?"

"Get your ass up here right now," I said and hung up before he could answer.

I'd just poured two glasses of red wine when there was a knock on my door.

He was loosening his tie when I opened it.

I grabbed it and pulled him into the room, slamming and locking the door behind him and then pressing him up against the door. He didn't argue.

13

The next morning when I woke, Anthony was gone.

He'd left me a note in nearly illegible handwriting saying he had meetings the rest of the day and would be catching a red-eye back to DC that night.

"Any chance you can come visit me this weekend?" the note said. "I miss you."

I felt the same way. I missed him already even though we'd just spent the night together. We hadn't really had a chance to talk.

I hadn't even told him what was going on with Clara.

I texted him that I'd try to come out in a few weeks.

Maybe by then I'd know who the real killer was.

"Don't forget to wear that necklace until I see you again," he wrote.

I fingered the solid gold Italian cornicello charm on the thick gold chain. He'd given it to me when he first arrived last night. I'd been about to drag him to bed when he stopped me and held out a small, black velvet box.

I'd opened it and smiled.

We were both Italian-American, and this was a gift that only a fellow paesano would appreciate. We rarely talked about our heritage, but I knew what the gold horn was—a talisman against the evil eye.

"You really do care?" I said in a half-mocking tone.

"You do know that for a cornicello to be effective, it has to be a gift from someone else?"

"No kidding?"

"Seriously," he said. "And it must also be worn at all times."

I leaned forward. "Even when I'm naked?"

"Especially when you're naked."

"Well, it is pretty," I said and admired it on my neck in the mirror by my front door.

Anthony, who was standing behind me, began to kiss the back of my neck.

"Let's make sure it looks good on you naked."

"Sounds like a plan."

I was still holding my phone and thinking of my night with Anthony when Darling texted me, reminding me about the memorial service. Talk about a somber reminder of my real life.

I texted Danny even though I knew he would still be asleep since it was before noon. I figured he was still digging around for info because if he'd found anything really important last night, he would've texted me before he went to sleep at dawn.

Then I decided I'd head over there in person. I hadn't seen him for a while.

I texted him again, saying to expect me at one that afternoon. I'd work out at the hotel gym, swim a few laps, and then show up at Danny's with a pizza from North Beach.

I dressed in my Lululemon black leggings and a tank top and headed to the VIP gym. When Dante and I had remodeled the hotel, we'd created a smaller gym for the four people who had penthouse suites to use. Our penthouse suites—each one located on a corner of the highest floor—had been the coup de grace in our remodel. They required a minimum stay of one week, and there was a vetting process. So far, we'd had assorted princes and billionaires and a celebrity or two. We'd marketed the penthouses as the ultimate luxury suites. Each came with a private chef, maid, and, if requested, a personal assistant. Each suite had its own elevator that led to a private garage underneath the building. And the rooftop helipad had a stairwell to each suite.

I logged onto my laptop to see who was staying in the penthouses this week. A tech tycoon. A sheik from Dubai. A K-pop star from Korea. An Instagram influencer.

Hopefully none of them felt like working out this morning. I wasn't feeling very social.

I was relieved to see the gym was empty.

I'd been working out for about an hour when the door opened, and I saw the handsome sheik enter. I gave him a slight nod, grabbed my towel, and was gone.

Shortly before one, I stood outside the building I'd once owned, juggling a large pizza box as I entered the door code. As soon as I was in front of Danny's steel reinforced door on the top floor, it swung open.

"Morning," he grumbled. He looked half asleep.

"Breakfast," I said and handed it to him as I walked in.

My old apartment brought back memories of Rose as a small girl. We'd lived here with James and Django, my sweet dog who would let himself out to do his business by hitting the button that opened the door to the rooftop terrace.

I'd been so happy living here.

But I'd been just as happy to turn it over to Danny.

He'd remodeled the loft and made it a hacker haven.

The small kitchen and bedroom was all that remained of the place I'd once lived in. The rest of the loft was now walled off into a dark cave that housed tables with banks of computers with red, blue, and green lights glowing and a persistent humming.

The door to the cave was open, but Danny headed to the kitchen and put down the pizza box.

"Want something to drink?" he said.

"I'm good," I said. "And I already ate, but feel free to dig in."

He hefted a slice, folded it in half lengthwise, and devoured it in seconds.

No surprise. Danny was six feet five inches tall and probably weighed nearly three bills. He had a disease that made him grow much too fast.

I'd paid a quarter of a million dollars for a new experimental drug that seemed to keep his growth spurts at bay. I was hoping it would keep him alive longer since most people with his disease died young.

He jutted his chin at the cave. "Want to see what I found?"

"Yeah."

Danny pulled up a bar stool and kicked another one toward me. He scooted his chair toward a large monitor.

"I'll stand," I said, moving closer.

He flicked the mouse, and pictures of the suspect popped up. A few were mugshots taken over the years. I looked at those first. He'd been arrested for stupid stuff—auto theft, shoplifting, warrants for speeding tickets he'd never paid. The worst was for a commercial burglary. He'd broken into—of all places—a toy store.

"What'd he steal?"

"A doll. An expensive doll. But a doll."

"Fuck," I said.

"I know."

I'd been hoping he was a total piece-of-shit drug addict, but the picture I was getting didn't jive. I looked at the other pictures. They looked like they'd been cribbed from someone's cell phone. They showed him as a younger man. He was standing with other young men, flashing gang signs and showing off gang tattoos.

"Where'd you find these?" I asked. "Myspace?"

"Ha ha," Danny said, clearly not amused. "Facebook. His ex-girlfriend has an account and likes to post there."

"Wait!" I said in a fake shocked voice. "You actually got on Facebook?"

I knew he thought the social media site was uncool.

"He doesn't seem good for it," Danny said.

I nodded and bit the inside of my lip, thinking.

He was right.

Something was wrong.

There was a man in custody for the quadruple homicide, but none of it made sense.

14

Dante had told me to wear my black wrap Diane Von Furstenberg dress to the memorial service, so that's what I did.

I didn't trust myself to dress appropriately for the service.

I mean, I knew not to wear jeans or my leather pants, but after a shower, I stared at the clothes in my closet for what felt like an hour before I called Dante. He didn't answer the phone, but ten minutes later, I got a text:

"The DVF dress. With your Jimmy Choo black pumps. You can bring your black cashmere shawl in case it gets cold. Wear your Burberry trench coat and just stick your keys and phone in the pockets. If you bring a purse, you'll probably lose it."

I stared at the text for a few seconds trying to figure out why he thought I'd lose a purse.

Maybe because I don't usually carry one? Finally, I gave up trying to read Dante's mind and got dressed.

The only thing that stumped me was whether to wear black tights with the outfit or go bare-legged. I texted Dante, and when he didn't answer, I just decided to go with the tights. I figured the less skin showing the better.

I cinched the belt on my trench coat, grabbed my keys and

phone, and headed downstairs to the garage. At the last minute, I realized I probably shouldn't ride my new motorcycle. I'd take the Maserati.

I got to the church a few minutes early and stood at the back, searching for Darling.

I tried not to look at the altar but couldn't help it. It was filled with bouquets of flowers and large poster boards with photos of Clara on them. One massive photo of her took center stage.

There wasn't a casket.

Darling had told me they weren't sure when they were going to be able to get Clara's body back, but the community needed a service so everyone could grieve.

When the coroner's office did release the body, a private funeral service would be held for close family only.

I spotted Darling toward the front. She was talking to someone I didn't recognize. She gestured for me to come over. I hugged her, and right away, a pastor came to the front of the church and asked everyone to be seated.

Most had settled into their seats when the back door blew open as if a gust of strong wind had forced it.

All the people in the pews turned to look at the man who walked in.

He had black hair shot with silver and a ruddy skin tone. He looked like he had once been attractive, but the sneer on his face reminded me of that saying that when you are young, you get the face your parents gave you, but after forty, you get the face you deserve.

He wore a Burberry trench coat. I could tell when I saw the distinctive plaid lining as he took off the coat and meticulously folded it over one arm.

Underneath he wore a dark blue pinstriped, three-piece suit that was obviously custom tailored. It looked like something

Dante would wear. And like Dante taught me, I glanced down at the man's shoes.

Italian leather. Custom made.

After twenty plus years as the best friend of an insanely fashionable gay man, I'd learned a thing or two. That didn't mean I always followed what I'd been taught, but I knew enough to immediately look at someone's shoes to see if they had money. That little tidbit of sleuthing often came in handy.

Darling made a small clicking noise that emerged from under her dark lace veil.

"Who is he?" I whispered.

"Clara's old boss. Big city attorney."

"You don't like him?"

Darling gave a long, exaggerated sigh.

"Just look at him. What's to like?"

She was right. He looked like a pompous prick. He had a mean face. I'd go so far as to say it was dickish. He was the type of man who would belittle service people. I knew it in my bones. Yep. Just from the way he walked into a room.

Someone tried to hand him a memorial leaflet, and he brushed them aside.

I bristled. I didn't like him. And I was having a hard time imagining sweet, bright, and conscientious Clara working for a man like that. If I ever found out he'd treated her badly, I'd step on his neck with the stiletto heel of my Jimmy Choo's.

I was lost in this thought and still staring at him when Darling nudged me.

"That's her daddy. He flew in from Brazil for the funeral."

I watched a handsome dark-skinned black man walk into the church and pause. As soon as his eyes took in the altar, he crumbled. It was as if he deflated before us. A petite woman in high heels and a tight beige dress, gripped his arm as if to try to support him. He leaned into her and she held him. She must be wife number two.

There was the sound of fabric rustling and whispers and then Clara's mother was up from her seat in the front row and hurrying to the back of the church where she enveloped both of them in a hug. Then she got on the other side of her ex-husband, who was openly weeping, and the two women helped him to the front of the church.

I watched in wonder.

What was up with these people? They forgave murderers and were kind to their exes and new spouse?

I didn't get it.

I watched Clara's boss get up from where he was sitting and walk to the front of the church to say something to Clara's mother. The music had already started, and people had all been seated so it seemed out of place and, frankly, rude.

He said something in a loud voice, but I couldn't make out his words.

He obviously thought he was so important he could barge up to the front of the church and speak to the family while the rest of us plebeians stayed in our seats.

After a few frantic-eyed glances were exchanged by the ushers, one of them came up and touched the man's elbow. He gave a small scowl and began to brush the other man aside when something was said to him from the row in front of him. He shook his head and tromped back to his seat.

I looked over at Darling, and her eyes were as wide as saucers. "Some people," she mouthed.

I tried not to laugh.

It was a moment of levity during an incredibly sad situation. She smiled back.

Then the preacher got up and talked about Clara.

I fought back tears the entire time.

I barely knew the girl. I had met her once.

It seemed contrived for me to cry, so I tried my best not to.

But it was fucking sad.

I thought about how I was going to have to tell Rose another person she knew had died violently.

As soon as I thought that, there was an outburst from the row where Clara's family sat.

An older woman wearing a black dress with a white collar and white gloves burst into loud weeping. All the other women around her tried to comfort her, speaking in soothing tones. The preacher paused and said, "It's okay, sister, you just let it out."

And the woman did, wailing even louder.

It was heartbreaking.

Darling began to sob loudly, and then it seemed everyone in the church was crying.

The older woman rocked back and forth making a keening noise.

It was too much.

I wanted to jump out of my seat and run away.

But Darling was clutching my hand desperately and mopping at the tears streaming down her face.

Then my sadness suddenly lifted and was replaced by fury.

These good women had had their hearts ripped out by the man I'd spoken to yesterday. He'd killed four innocent young people who had their lives in front of them.

I got down on my knees, put my hands together, looked at the cross hanging in the front of the church, and I said my own prayer.

I hadn't prayed for years. I'd felt abandoned by God since my parents had been murdered.

But for some reason, I found myself on my knees praying for my own soul.

"God, forgive me for what I'm going to do when I find out who killed Clara," I murmured.

"Oh, dear Lord, forgive her, for she knows not what she says," Darling said beside me. "You're not going to do anything except call the police. Right, Gia?"

I closed my eyes. Darling and her bionic ears had heard my whispered words.

Then the preacher finished his prayer with a hearty "Amen," and we all stood.

Just in time.

After the service, we all filed out of the sanctuary and into a cafeteria downstairs where there were tables filled with food—pasta dishes, tuna casseroles, meat and cheese trays, and an entire long table just with desserts.

I followed Darling to a table and sat down beside her.

She seemed so deflated. It was hard to see her like that.

"Let me fix you a plate," I said, hovering over her.

"I can't eat," she said.

That worried me. Darling loved food. Loved it.

"Maybe a little piece of pie?" I urged.

"No. I just can't, Gia."

I patted her silk-clad shoulder. "Okay."

I sank into the chair beside her, feeling useless.

Then the family came in. Clara's mother looked like royalty, holding her head high. But two women on each side of her clutched her arms.

"Her sisters," Darling said.

We watched them walk toward another table and stand near the chairs. They placed their handbags on the seats but didn't sit.

A line quickly formed as people walked over to pay their respects.

"We can go last," Darling said.

I watched Clara's boss make his way to the front, obliviously cutting off other people and barging through those going slower than him.

What a douche.

He said something to Clara's mother and then turned to leave. He was heading for the door.

I was out of my seat. "You okay if I take off? I just thought of something."

She smiled. "Mmmhmm. I'm fine, baby. You go on."

"It's about Clara's killer." I felt I owed her the truth.

"I heard your prayer in church, Gia. It concerns me."

"Don't worry about me," I said.

"Remember, they don't want your type of justice, Gia," she said. "You gotta respect that."

"It's hard."

I watched as the attorney was pulled to the side to speak to someone. I needed to hurry.

Darling's eyes grew steely. "I want him dead, too, baby. Don't you ever forget that. I want him strung up and killed slowly and painfully."

I kissed her on the forehead and then made my way as quickly as I could to the door where the attorney had slipped out.

As soon as I was in the hallway and out of sight, I ran.

The hall led to an exit door. I burst out of it in time to see a black BMW leaving the parking lot. I memorized the license plate and pulled out my phone.

"James? Can you run this plate for me?"

I reeled off the numbers and letters, then I hung up and headed for my own car.

I still had a chance to catch up to him. I wanted to see where he was heading. I didn't trust the guy for one second.

It was only a hunch, but my hunches were usually damn good.

I didn't catch up to the BMW. I was about to get in my car when there was a commotion from the church. I heard screams, so I raced back inside, wishing I'd not listened to Dante's instructions and had brought my gun.

Inside the church, a small crowd was gathered in front of the altar. I pushed my way through to find an elderly woman propped up on a pew with a man checking her pulse.

I found Darling, and she whispered. "It's all good. Grandma Laverne fainted."

"Mama, I told you not to come back into the church by yourself," I heard one woman say.

"I wanted to see my grandbaby. You can't stop me from seeing her."

"Mama, she's not even here, remember?"

The woman looked around, confused. "Where did you hide her casket? You're hiding it from me, aren't you? I just want to see Clara one last time. You can't deny me that."

The older woman began to cry.

Then the woman crouched at her feet began to cry too.

Darling headed over. "Grandma Laverne. You come with me. We're going to go see Clara now."

"We are?"

"Yes, ma'am."

Oh shit. What was Darling going to do now?

We all watched as she helped the woman up and took her arm. "Come on, now. Let's go."

The woman smiled and turned back to the younger woman. "See? Darling said I could."

"That's good, mama," the woman said with a sigh. "You go on now."

Darling led Grandma Laverne to the altar, speaking in a low voice. "Look at Clara as a baby here," she said and pointed to a picture. "Wasn't she just the cutest little bug?"

"She sure was," the older woman said.

As Darling pointed at pictures and spoke, the older woman calmed.

Meanwhile, the small group that had surrounded Grandma Laverne were now huddled in a hug, weeping.

I backed away, trying not to make any sound.

I decided to leave the family in peace and headed back out to my car.

It had nothing to do with the tears running down my face. Nothing at all.

15

When I arrived at the jail the next day, there was a woman and a little girl using a walker in line. I got behind them.

The woman had on a floral dress and flip flops. The girl was wearing pajama pants and slippers and had deep, black circles under her eyes. She looked very sickly.

Just then the woman's phone rang.

She turned to the girl. "Honey, go sit down."

The girl did as she was told. She sat on a bench and began to swing her legs while staring down at a cell phone.

When the woman turned I saw the slip she'd filled out to visit an inmate.

The name on the slip said Robert Enzenauer.

"I'm about to go see him," the woman in front of me said in a low voice. "I just told Trisha to go sit down so she doesn't hear."

I scooted as close as I could without being up in their business.

"Mama, the money just appeared in the account for Trisha's surgery."

Holy fuck.

The woman lowered her voice to a whisper, but I heard every word:

"It's blood money, mama. It's a sin to use that kind of money."

I heard a woman's voice on the other end of the phone but couldn't make out what she was saying.

I eyed the line. Fuck. It was growing shorter. I needed to hear more before the woman got to the counter.

"I'm about to go ask him. He won't tell me though. He just looks at me all sad. That's why I know. It's a deal with the devil," she looked around, and I quickly looked down at my boots.

Then I clearly heard the woman's voice on the other end of the phone.

"Kanisha, you take that money, and you don't say a damn word. I'm calling Dr. Gilles right now and telling him to schedule the surgery as soon as possible. He wanted to do it tomorrow. I'm going to see if he can get her in for the pre-surgery stuff today. You want your daughter to live or die? You don't have a choice."

"Okay, mama. Okay. I'm leaving now. I'll come see him after it's over. Tell him it went well. But then I'm done. I'm filing for divorce. I can't be married to a murderer."

The woman burst into tears and then surprised me by stepping out of the line and walking over to the girl.

"Come on, Trisha, we're going to go see Dr. Gilles. You're going to have that surgery."

"Really, mama? Really?" the girl said. Her face lit up with a big smile.

The woman wiped her tears away and said, "Really."

"What about daddy?" the girl said, hesitating.

"We'll see him after the surgery, okay?"

The girl seemed reluctant to leave.

"Come on. Grandma is calling Dr. Gilles right now. We want to see how soon we can get you in, okay, sweet baby?"

"Okay, mama."

I was at the front of the line now. I wondered if the clerk recognized me. It was the same woman from the day before. If so, she didn't say anything. She looked bored out of her mind. I was sure she got to deal with some really fun people in her position.

She handed me back my ID and told me to go sit.

This time when I walked in, Robert Enzenauer was standing.

"I thought I told you I didn't want to talk to you."

I smiled.

"Listen, I came back because I found out that you're actually not the total monster I thought. I mean you're still a fucking monster." I paused and he moved to hang up the phone so I quickly said the rest: "But I know you did it all for Trisha."

HIs pale face grew even paler. "How do you know my daughter's name?"

I noticed he didn't deny my statement.

"She needs that surgery," I said. "I know you were desperate to save her life. I get that. I don't know who paid you to kill Clara and her friends, but you are going to tell me."

He had regained his composure. He narrowed his eyes.

"I ain't telling you shit."

"Who hired you?"

He spit on the ground.

I tried to ignore it.

"Are you worried if you tell me something will happen to your family? Will the money be taken back? What's your concern? You're already going to prison for life or getting the death penalty. Your kid is already going to get the surgery. The way I see it, you have nothing to lose by telling me who paid you."

He looked up at the camera in the corner.

"You are afraid," I said. "And the only reason you'd be afraid is for your family, right? Unless you're a total pussy and are worried about someone shanking you in prison, and it's a little late to worry about that."

He sneered. "I ain't afraid of nobody in this place. Nobody."

"You probably should be," I said lightly and then said, "Listen, tell me who paid you? If I kill them, they can't hurt your family. I have no beef with your wife and little girl. They deserve to live. But the person who hired you? He is going to die."

He shook his head.

"You know," he said. "You're as dumb as you look. You know this whole time we're being recorded, right?"

"That's why you won't talk?" I asked. "Well, why should I worry? If you're telling the truth, then my threat to kill the person who hired you is an empty threat, right? You can't kill someone who doesn't exist."

He rolled his eyes.

Real mature.

"So thank you," I said, "for confirming you were just a stupid little hit man hired to do a job. It makes more sense now. You don't look smart enough to plan those murders on your own anyway."

"Fuck you, bitch!" He stood again and was reaching to hang up the phone when I spoke quickly.

"I'm not kidding about a deal. Me and you. I'll take him out so he can't ever hurt your family. I *want* to take him out. I'm ready to take him out for Clara's murder. I can't get to you, so I'm going to get to him."

He froze, his eyes on mine.

"I'm dead serious," I said into the phone. "Just give me his name."

"My lawyer told me not to talk to you anymore."

"You've been talking to me all night," I said. I was watching his eyes, and he was making weird eye motions at me. I didn't get it for a second. Then he spoke again.

"My *lawyer* said."

This time he emphasized "lawyer" in a really weird way.

"Your lawyer?"

"Yes. My lawyer. He said not to talk to you anymore. If you want to argue, you can take it up with him."

"Who's your lawyer?"

Then he grinned. A big-ass toothy grin. And hung up the phone.

Fuck me.

16

Once I was in my car, I dialed James.

"Yo."

"Yo yourself," I said.

"He just gave up his lawyer as the guy who hired him to take out a hit on Clara and her friends."

"That makes zero sense."

I relayed my jailhouse conversation.

"Stand by," James said.

I heard him clicking on a keyboard.

"He doesn't have a lawyer. He said he didn't need one. He was going to plead guilty and represent himself."

"What the fuck? That reinforces what I think—that he was sending me a message by emphasizing 'lawyer.'"

"If you figure out who he's talking about, let me know."

James hung up.

Within thirty seconds, I knew.

That douchebag from the funeral.

I called James back.

"The attorney Clara worked for last summer. She was an intern."

James exhaled loudly.

"What?"

"Same guy you had me run plates on? His name is Jeffrey Phillips."

"Yes!" I said, my voice filled with excitement.

"That's a problem.

"Excuse me?"

"He's the DA's brother."

"Bullshit."

"Not kidding."

No wonder the dude in jail was laughing at me. The man who hired him was untouchable.

Or at least appeared to be.

"I don't care if he's the Attorney General's brother; he's a killer." I went through the toll booth for the Richmond bridge and accelerated across the water to the road that would lead me right past San Quentin.

"It's going to be a hard case to build when the DA's reluctant to prosecute."

I took a curve a little too fast and my tires squealed. I was thinking hard.

"Wouldn't the crime be prosecuted in the county where the bodies were found?"

"Not if they were killed in San Francisco."

I glanced over at the Golden Gate and the Bay Bridge off to my left.

They'd left the club and, after that, nobody knew where they went.

"What about Find My phone and other fucking apps that track every goddamn move we make?" I asked. "There were four twenty somethings in a car—something had to track them in some way. It is inconceivable that all four had phones completely off the grid."

"True. I'll tell Hicks to make sure he's not letting that point slip in his investigation. He's pretty old school."

I was passing San Quentin now and peered over at it, wondering if the cars pulling out were full of baby mamas and elderly mother's and childhood friends.

"Back to the DA. Is he really so corrupt that he would allow his brother to get away with murder?"

"Let's just say there have been instances in the past that seemed a little shady."

"Spill it."

James went on to tell me a story about when the brothers had been students at UC Berkeley, and one of them had been accused of date rape. The other had acted as an alibi.

"What a piece of shit."

"There's more," James said.

Apparently, Phillips brother was also accused of cheating in school, and somehow that accusation disappeared.

The DA brother also arranged to have some misdemeanor charges dismissed and the records sealed.

"Did all this come out when he ran for the office?" I asked. "I don't remember it being a contentious race."

"Big brother made it all go away."

"Really? How would he do that?"

"Good question. An investigative reporter had a story ready to go and called big brother for a quote. The next day, the story was killed, and the reporter quit and suddenly moved away."

"Give me that reporter's name."

"Hold up. It will take me some digging to find it. And the only reason I even know the name is that I saved an article she wrote on hackers."

"Of course you did."

I took the turn to the Golden Gate bridge and rolled up my

car window as I drove onto it. There was a wicked cold wind blowing in from the Pacific Ocean.

17

I slid deeper into my car seat and pulled my face back a little into my thick hoodie as a man walked by, glancing curiously into my window.

I exhaled as he continued without stopping or giving me a second look.

I was parked outside Jeffrey Phillip's law firm watching the door and waiting for him to come out.

The street was well lit and fairly busy. People walked past on their way to the shops and restaurants closer to the Embarcadero, the street that lined the waterfront to the city's east.

Terminal Island, nestled under the Bay Bridge, began to light up as homeowners returned to the small residential area on the island.

I was dying for a cigarette. I tried not to smoke, but the craving was always there. Especially when I was bored and had to sit still for hours on end. Every once in a while, I turned on the engine to generate some heat but didn't leave it on long in case it kicked out exhaust or something else that gave away I was in the car.

If I leaned down a little, I could peer up at the top floor

where the law firm was located and see that all the office lights were still on.

How late did they work?

I'd been there for three hours. I'd shown up at five, thinking that it would be a reasonable time for Jeffrey Phillips and his staff to go home. Instead of people coming out, a livery car dropped off a group of four men in suits who went into the building.

The car sped away, and the men were inside within seconds.

Taking a chance I'd blow my cover, I quickly ran inside the lobby in time to see the elevator doors whoosh closed. The men had gone to the top floor, which was dominated by Jeffrey Phillips's law firm.

Interesting.

I closed my eyes, trying to picture the men I'd seen go inside.

All four wore expensive-looking gray suits. All four had neatly trimmed dark hair about the same length, and all four wore sunglasses.

In other words, they all looked alike. I couldn't think of one distinguishing trait among them.

My aunt Eva, the Queen of Spades, had told me to practice skills training my brain to develop a photographic memory.

But I couldn't for the life of me picture even one of the men's faces.

I was debating whether to take the elevator up to the law firm and make up some story or stay in my car when I saw the elevator start to come back down from the top floor. I raced back to my car and was safely inside when a tall, slim woman with gazelle-like legs and brown hair in a huge bun came out the front door. She was carrying a Louis Vuitton suitcase-sized bag and walked gracefully on Christian Louboutin stilettos. At first I thought she might be a law partner until I saw her hail a cab. A partner would have her own driver.

As the cab drove away, I wondered who was still upstairs at the law firm besides the four men.

It seemed that the minute they arrived, this woman left.

I waited to find out.

It was nine o'clock, and I was dying of boredom before the front door opened again.

The four men emerged and seconds later the livery car pulled up.

They were inside the vehicle before I could react. I memorized the license plate number and then started my engine. I was about to follow the car when I remembered that my target was still inside.

I texted James the license plate number without explanation and sat back, enjoying the warmth of the heater blowing on my cold hands.

A few minutes later, the door to the building's underground garage opened, and a yellow Lamborghini Urus zipped out. Such a strange car. It looked like a souped up Prius with an ugly paint job. I waited a beat and then pulled onto the street behind it.

I stayed a few cars back as the person in the Lambo navigated San Francisco streets, making its way to Union Street. The driver pulled off the street and in front of a restaurant so fast that a valet jumped back from the curb. The young man regained his composure and raced over to open the door. I waited until I saw Phillips get out of the car. I crept forward until I could see in the windows of the restaurant. I ignored the cars behind me, honking as I stayed stopped in the street. Phillips strode in and straight to a table where a delicate looking woman with bright red hair sat. He leaned down to kiss her cheek. She turned her head and his kiss landed on her hair. Mrs. Phillips?

His face reddened, and a frown knit his eyebrows together. His mouth opened and what he was saying was obviously loud because the people at the next table looked over. The woman stood. She was tall and somewhat emaciated with very thin legs sticking out of a pencil skirt. She wore a Chanel jacket and a thick choker of pearls on her long neck. Phillips ignored her and sat down, grabbing a menu and sticking it in front of his face.

I lost sight of the woman for a few seconds. A parking spot across the street from the restaurant opened up, so I did a little trick I learned in a Skip Barber racing school class and did a quick reverse ninety-degree turn into it.

The driver who had been honking behind me a few seconds earlier, slowed, rolled down his window and did a slow clap before driving away.

That's when I caught sight of the woman again. She was now out on the sidewalk with what looked like a cashmere beige coat tightly wrapped around her. The valet had just pulled up with a beige Mercedes when Phillips came out.

I got out of my car, crossed the street and lit a cigarette while standing in front of the coffee shop next door.

"Come on, Jenny, you're being ridiculous. I had a late meeting. Like I told you."

I could hear every word.

Jenny turned to him, and I held my breath waiting for her response.

"Maybe you weren't fucking your whore these past few hours, but don't you dare lie to me and tell me your meeting after dinner isn't with her. Don't. You. Dare."

"Jenny, we've gone over this. Sabina is just a friend. She's going to review the Cushman contract for me. We need to move on it tomorrow."

Jenny turned to him and gave a hysterical laugh.

"Oh fuck off, Jeffrey. I'm filing divorce papers in the morning. I can't take any more."

Just then, the manager came out.

"Sir, your jacket?" he held out a Burberry trench.

"God damn it, you idiot," Phillips said, turning his fury on the poor man. "If I wanted my jacket, I would've asked you for it!"

The maître d' didn't say a word, just turned on one heel and walked back inside.

"You are such an ass," the redhead said and turned toward the Mercedes.

Now, the gloves were off. Phillips's face contorted, and he grabbed her arm so forcibly, it jerked her around to face him.

"You will do no such thing. You will lose everything. Everything. I will make sure you never see your children again."

The woman remained strikingly poised and calm and slowly extracted her arm from his grip.

"I think you mean our children."

"What?" he said and seemed confused.

"Our children. You said 'your' children," she said. "They are *our* children, and you will pay every last penny to give them the life they are entitled to. If you dare to protest one single line of the divorce settlement, I will go to the police with everything I know."

I froze.

Phillips leaned forward and put his face close to his wife's and said in a low growl, "If you do, I will kill you."

The woman took a step back and very calmly and methodically raised her thin arm and slapped Phillips across the face.

"Go to hell," she said.

He stood with his mouth open in shock as she climbed into the Mercedes.

As she drove away, he stood there, watching and rubbing his cheek.

A valet came up to him.

"Should I get your car, sir?"

"Did I fucking ask you to get my car you little waste of space piece of shit?"

The man shook his head.

"Get lost!"

The valet scurried away. I shrank into the shadows of a nearby doorway.

Phillips gave a loud, cackling laugh.

"Dumb bitch just dug her own grave."

18

Phillips started walking my way.

Shit. He could recognize me.

We had been at the memorial service together. But I looked a lot different then. I'd been dressed up in stilettos with my hair down and makeup done. Now I had my hair in a ponytail and was wearing a hoodie and a motorcycle jacket with thick, steel-toed boots.

But I didn't want to take any chances.

I froze, waiting to see what he would do next.

He walked right up to me.

"Can I bum a smoke?"

I nodded, wide-eyed and handed him my pack.

I expected him to take one out, but he took the whole pack and then put one of the cigarettes in his mouth.

"Light?" he said, as if I was a dipshit for not anticipating his every move.

I smiled and leaned forward, opening my beat-up Zippo lighter.

Once his cigarette was lit, he smiled around it and said, "Good girl."

. . .

I WANTED to throat punch him, but restrained myself.

And I was glad I did because a few seconds later, he stepped a few feet away and took out his phone.

"Sabina? I'm coming over in a few minutes so be ready."

I couldn't hear the voice on the other end, but Phillips gave a low chuckle.

His voice lowered and he said, "I want to fuck you so hard you won't be able to walk for a week."

He glanced over at me. I didn't hide that I was staring at him and it was obvious I'd heard every word. His eyebrows raised in surprise.

"Be ready," he repeated and hung up.

Then he turned to me.

"You know you wish you had a man who talked to you like that, don't you?" he said, eyeing me. "You know, you're not half bad looking. If you didn't dress like a dyke, you might even be fuckable. Your face is spectacular, but you dress like a fucking homeless dude."

It would only take a second for me to break his neck. A second.

But I needed proof that he was behind Clara's murder.

"I bet you get a lot of tail," I said, exhaling my smoke right in his face.

He didn't flinch.

"You're a ballsy bitch to talk to me that way."

"Who else do you fuck? Your wife? Your mistress? Your secretary?"

"I fuck anyone I want," he said and this time it was his turn to exhale his smoke in my eyes. I didn't blink.

"I'd never fuck you," I said. "Not if my life was on the line."

His eyes narrowed.

"I can make that happen," he said in a dangerously low voice.

I laughed.

"You're too much of a pussy to kill someone," I said.

He laughed and said, "You'd be surprised."

My cigarette was now barely a stub.

I ground out the cigarette butt on the sidewalk.

"Nah. You're a fucking poser. I mean, I believe you'd hire a killer, but you'd never have the balls to kill someone yourself."

He took a step back.

I brushed past him and was gone.

19

When I got back to my hotel, I was shaking.

And not from the chill I'd gotten while staking out Phillips.

I was furious and a little shaken up by my encounter outside the restaurant.

The guy was a fucking douchebag, but something about him was dangerous.

And I'd played my hand.

I waited for him to go back inside the restaurant before turning around and racing back to my car.

I didn't want him to know what I drove.

I didn't want him to know anything about me.

He was a wimp, but he also was in a rare position of power and wasn't afraid to abuse it.

With his DA brother and his money and connections, he was potentially a threat.

One I could handle, but one I didn't dare underestimate.

I stripped down and took a hot shower to warm up, then wrapped in a fuzzy robe, and poured some bourbon to heat up my insides.

It burned down my throat into my belly.

The room service meal I'd ordered was waiting outside my door.

I sat down and ate my salmon, asparagus, and garlic mashed potatoes as I hunted for information on Mrs. Phillips.

I didn't need to use my limited hacker skills to find out that she was a skilled fundraiser in the city of San Francisco. She served on all kinds of old-fashioned boards for old money WASPs. She wasn't the president of any of the boards, I noted. She was always somewhere in the background, quietly doing her part, dripping in diamonds and designers, such as Chanel and Hermès. She was classy and beautiful, in a tired way.

I found pictures of her and Phillips when they were first married.

She'd been stunning in her thirties.

Her looks had been phenomenal until just last year. I studied the pictures, wondering how someone had aged that quickly. Maybe realizing what a douche she was married to had done it. I couldn't find anything in the news about any tragedy.

A tragedy could age someone overnight.

But the only difference I could find was that she had lost a lot of weight.

When I compared pictures at an annual charity ball between this year and last, I could see she'd lost some thirty pounds. And it did not suit her. I wondered if she'd lost weight because she was ill, but digging deeper, I found an article about how she'd been seen with a celebrity weight loss expert and pictures of her at the gym.

I supposed finding out her husband was having an affair could have motivated her to lose weight she didn't need to lose.

Being so thin made her seem sickly and older.

It reminded me of what Catherine Deneuve had once said: "Either your face or your ass."

Luckily, I'd never been concerned about not having a rather

large badonkadonk. It would have been stupid and futile to worry about that. And the older I got, the more I realized that it was an asset. No pun intended.

After my meal, I closed my laptop and headed toward my minibar.

I poured another few fingers of the bourbon and took the glass out on the deck with me.

The wind whipped my hair as I leaned on the rail, looking down at the city and called James.

"It's him. I guarantee it."

"Where's your proof?"

"I overheard him arguing with his wife. She threatened to divorce him, and he started playing dirty. He said he'd keep the kids. She said she'd go to the police about something. He said he'd kill her. I fucking heard it, James."

"I believe you."

We both sat there in silence for a few seconds.

"We've got to turn the wife," he said.

"I agree."

"I can bring her in," he said. "I can offer her witness protection."

I thought about the woman in Chanel driving the Mercedes.

"She's not going to settle for some three-bedroom rambler in a small Kansas town," I said. "She's going to want Rio or something. Or a fucking yacht. I don't know. I mean, I'm willing to pitch in, but it's going to cost you Feebs a bundle."

"Pitch in?" James scoffed. "It's a fucking federal program, Gia. It's not like you're offering to give me some gas money on a road trip."

"I can do that too."

But I knew he was right.

"I'll go up the ladder and see how much they care."

"About four black young people murdered in a field with the

cops saying it's a drug deal gone bad?"

He didn't answer. The wind died down, and it actually felt pleasant out on my deck.

Goddamn it. I'd have to go talk to Mrs. Phillips on my own.

"Let's meet with Hicks," he said after a long pause. "I called him earlier, and he gave me an old code word that meant he couldn't talk on the phone."

"That's fucking weird."

"I know," James said. "That's why we need to meet in person. What are you doing tomorrow afternoon?"

"Name the time."

"I'll plan on picking you up at three unless I hear differently from Hicks."

"Thanks, James." I said it in a softer voice. I knew he was doing all this for me. He had bigger and more important cases to deal with.

"I got your back, Gia. Always have. Always will."

I hung up before the damn fool made me cry.

The sound of a helicopter grew louder, and I could feel the vibration of the rotors in my bones as it came in to land on the rooftop helipad. Must be one of the big honchos staying in our penthouse suites. I usually was a little more on top of who our guests were, but I'd been so absorbed in finding out who killed Clara that I'd let my hotel responsibilities slide. It was fine.

That's why I had such a rock star team in place. I didn't need to micromanage every last thing. I'd handpicked all the managers, so they could run the show without me.

Even so, I did feel a trickle of guilt race over me.

Maybe I'd put on a fancy dress and drop by the restaurant bar to say hi to the guests. It would be a good distraction until tomorrow when I planned to make an early brunch visit to Mrs. Phillips.

I might even bring donuts.

20

I was worried James would try to stop me, so I didn't ask him for the Phillips's home address.

Instead I turned to my secret weapon—Danny.

The Philips's lived in the Sea Cliff neighborhood. Not the richest neighborhood in the city, but it was right up there. After Danny texted me the address, I searched it online and saw the house last sold for $15 million. It seemed like a hell of a lot for an attorney to pay, but what did I know?

I called Dante.

"Can a top attorney afford a $15 million house in the city?" I asked.

"How about, 'Hi, Dante. How are you and Wayne?'"

"Yeah. Yeah. All the pleasantries. Now what do you think?"

"When you say top attorney what do you mean?"

"Never mind," I said in frustration. "I'm just looking for corruption. I was hoping he wouldn't have been able to buy it legally, you know?"

"This is about Darling's niece's murder, isn't it?"

"No," I said quickly. "Hey, I've got to go. Nice talking to you."

I hung up before he could answer.

I studied the picture of the house.

It was painted coral, had a two-car garage, and faced the Golden Gate Bridge—more than faced it... There was nothing between the house and the bridge except water.

I scanned the details. The monthly mortgage was $65,000, but it would only rent for $42,000 a month. Maybe not a great investment.

Then it sunk in what type of website I was looking at. A real estate site. The house was for sale. It was a new listing.

Holy shit. Was he fleeing the country?

I decided to wait until about 10:00 a.m. to go visit Mrs. Phillips.

By then, Jeffrey Phillips would hopefully be fully engaged in work at his law firm, even if he had slept in.

I pulled right into the driveway, figuring *What the hell?*

A frosted glass window revealed movement as someone responded to me ringing the doorbell.

I smiled at the peephole. I'd dressed in baggy jogger pants, a hoodie, and white sneakers. I'd pulled my hair back in a ponytail and skipped the makeup. I wanted to appear unthreatening and hopefully disarm her into trusting me.

Mrs. Phillips opened the door.

"Are you the cleaning lady I ordered?" Her eyes barely skimmed over me before she was looking over my shoulder.

Ordered. Like a package. I guess I did appear unthreatening.

"Sure," I said. She frowned but opened the door wider. I didn't wait for an invite and made my way inside.

The entire house was empty. Boxes were stacked in one corner of a great room.

"The cleaning supplies are in here," she said, pointing to a room off the kitchen.

I pulled myself up onto the kitchen counter. I pushed aside a manila folder. The corner of a piece of paper showing a flight itinerary peeked out.

"Where are you moving?"

"Excuse me?"

I used one fingernail to flip open the manila folder and glanced down.

"Ah. Nice, France. The old French Riviera," I said. "I have a good friend who lives there. A really good friend, if you know what I mean."

"Who are you?" As she spoke, she eyed a cell phone on the counter near me. I picked it up and casually tossed it into a mop bucket full of water near my feet.

She gasped and backed up.

"I'm not here to hurt you. I am actually here to help you," I said. "The only person I'm interested in hurting is your husband."

I paused to see her reaction.

There was none.

I admired her composure.

"I have no idea what you're talking about."

Her eyes did something strange. Instead of looking at me, she looked off to a doorway to my right.

"Listen, I know he killed—well not with his bare hands, but same diff—killed four people."

I paused again.

"It's time for you to leave," she said. I'll call the police."

"I'm really on your side," I tried again. "If he's in jail, he can't hurt your kids or take them away from you. Or leave you destitute, right?"

"You are insane. Leave my house right now."

She shouted the words this time and looked off to the doorway to the right again.

Suddenly I realized why.

We weren't alone.

A second later, Jeffrey Phillips walked in and without even looking at me, came up behind her and wrapped his arms around her waist, kissing her neck.

Then he drew back.

"Oh, we have company," he said and gave me a tight smile. "Who is this?"

"She was applying to be the new nanny in France. But I don't think she's a good fit."

"She's not," he said. "I'll walk her out."

Just then, two kids ran in.

One was a boy about six and the other a girl about four.

"Is she our new nanny?" the little girl asked, twirling on one foot.

Jenny laughed. "No. She's the housecleaner. Can't you tell?"

The boy gave me the once over and turned up his nose. "Yeah. She smells funny."

The woman laughed. "We're done here," she said. "Don't ever contact me again. If you do, I'll file a restraining order against you. As you know, I'm connected to one of the most powerful attorneys in the world."

I gave her a tight smile. "I feel sorry for you. I hope he paid you enough blood money to live with the knowledge that you are partly responsible for destroying the lives of four families."

She laughed. "Oh, you really are insane."

Phillips gripped my elbow. "Time to leave."

I shook off his hand and grabbed his forearm, twisting it.

"Daddy!" the little girl said.

I released my grip.

"I'll walk you out now," he growled.

"You first."

He bit his lip and headed toward the door.

He swung it open and stepped outside. I followed him, keeping my distance.

He reached over and slammed the door shut.

Once we were alone, he leaned forward.

I held up a hand. "Any closer and I break your nose. If you don't think I can do it, go ahead and try me."

He stayed where he was.

"Who the fuck are you, and what are you doing in my house?" he said in a low growl.

"You're going down," I said. "I know you hired Enzenauer to kill Clara and her friends. And I'm going to make sure you pay."

21

I was in front of the hotel right at three when James pulled up in his Crown Vic.

"Yo," I said, hopping in.

"Hey," he said. He seemed distracted. He barely even looked at me.

"Everything okay?"

"No," he said. "Ever since her mom died of breast cancer and they found Janie had the same genetic marker, they've had her do special 3D ultrasounds each year. This morning they found something they were concerned about and scheduled a biopsy."

"Oh fuck," I said and reached for the door handle. "Let's reschedule. Go be with her."

I unclicked my seatbelt.

He reached over and took my hand. "Thanks. But she's stubborn. She went to work. Said we won't know anything until we see the doctor in two weeks."

"Two weeks?" I said. "Fuck that. Let's find someone who can see her sooner."

"I don't—"

I cut him off. "I'll handle it."

He pulled out of the driveway and headed for the entrance to the freeway.

I started making phone calls. Finally, I reached a doctor who had known my mother back in the day. He was no longer practicing, but he knew someone who was and who would see Janie in two days. By the time I hung up, we'd just crossed the Bay Bridge and were cruising up the coast toward Richmond. From there, we'd cut across to Benicia where we were meeting Hicks at a diner.

"Thanks, Gia," James said.

"It's probably nothing," I said finally.

"Yeah, that's what Janie said."

We were quiet for a few moments and then I decided it was confession time.

"I went to visit Jenny Phillips yesterday."

James hit the steering wheel with his fist. "You're fucking kidding me."

"Nope. Mr. Phillips was there. They were getting along great. She's totally drunk the Kool Aid."

"Of course she did."

"And their house was packed. They're moving to France. I saw a plane ticket for tomorrow morning."

"Jesus."

"I thought you should know."

"Damn right I should know."

He reached for his phone.

Whoever James called was told to look for the Phillips family at the airport in the morning—all airlines with flights to France.

"Are you going to try to stop them?"

"I can't."

"Oh."

"Why are you upset?" I asked.

"Maybe you spooked them."

"Maybe. But their house was already listed and packed up when I arrived."

"He's looking more and more good for it."

"I know. What can we do about it?"

"We?"

"Yeah," I said, crossing my arms over my chest. "We."

"Law enforcement investigators can't find evidence that he was behind the murders."

"What if I find proof?"

"If you do find evidence, you need to immediately turn it over to the authorities."

"Oh my god," I said. "Could you sound any stuffier or more official?"

I rolled my eyes.

"Probably," he said and laughed.

We pulled into a strip mall in Benicia.

There was a small storefront with a sign that said "The Cobblestone Cafe."

"Hope they have grits," I said.

"What?" James said, making a face.

"You know—grits."

"I would bet my left nut that you've never tasted grits in your life."

I slammed the car door.

"Your future children are safe. I have never had grits. I never said I had. I just said I hope they have them."

"Gia," he said, completely ignoring what I was talking about. "Don't tell Hicks you visited Mrs. Phillips."

"Really?"

"Really."

James held the door open for me, and I leaned over and kissed his cheek to show no hard feelings. "Deal."

Hicks was sitting in a seat near the window with *his back to the door.*

What kind of cop was he?

We slid into the booth seat opposite him.

"Sheriff," I said with a nod.

"Ms. Santella."

The waitress came over and asked for our drink order.

All three of us ordered coffee.

After she walked away, James cleared his throat.

"Anything new from the autopsy reports?"

"We are rushing toxicology."

"Good," James said.

The waitress appeared with our coffee. I tried it. Bitter. But I was tired, so I sucked it down.

"Can I take your order?" she asked.

"Two eggs over easy, bacon, and sourdough toast," Hicks said.

"Same," I said.

"Make that three," James said.

James and Hicks started talking about some colleague of theirs who had died of a heart attack the day after he retired.

I interrupted. I wasn't there to walk down memory lane.

"They won't find any drugs in the tox report," I said.

Hicks nodded. "Maybe not."

James cleared his throat. "We wanted to meet with you because it looks like Phillips might be good for a murder-for-hire rap."

"God damn," Hicks said. "We have a better chance of indicting the governor of California."

"I know," James said.

"We'd need rock solid proof," Hicks said.

The waitress placed three plates in front of us. Fastest service I'd ever had. I looked over at the window leading to the kitchen and saw three faces staring back at us. Guess they were bored. We were the only ones in the place.

"I'm talking about irrefutable proof he hired the guy," Hicks said again.

"We're working on it," James said. God bless him.

"The problem is, I'm getting some pressure from up high," Hicks said, digging into his eggs.

My fork froze in midair.

"They want the case closed yesterday. Drug deal went bad. Bam."

I closed my eyes. *Fuck.*

"Who is working for you?" James asked.

"Not sure. The county board is standing as a united front. They said the board wants the investigation closed. Said it's bringing the county bad publicity and they want it buried before our annual gala fundraiser. It's the big money maker. Half of the county's residents live off what they make during the ten days of the fair. If word spreads about the homicides, it could hurt attendance. The fair opens in two weeks. They want the investigation closed in a week."

"So it's all about the money?" I asked.

"That's what they say," Hicks said. "But I think there's more to it. I think someone on the board is on the payroll and talked the others into this flimsy reason."

"Interesting," James said.

"It's bullshit," I said at the same time.

Hicks mopped his egg yolk up with a piece of toast and stuffed it in his mouth. I watched his mustache move up and down as he chewed. When he was done and swallowed, he looked right at me and said, "That gives you a week to find your evidence."

He slapped a one hundred dollar bill on the table, stood,

hitched up his pants and walked to the door. He waited outside, lighting a cigar while James and I gathered our things.

"A week, huh?" I said as soon as I walked out.

"Yeah."

"Okay then," I said.

22

James was quiet most of the way home.

When he dropped me off, I squeezed his hand.

"Keep me posted on what the doctor says Friday."

"We will."

I headed upstairs to my hotel suite. Once I was there I paced the deck outside, thinking.

I needed to figure out how to prove that Phillips was behind the murders.

Danny had given me the names of all of Phillips's employees the day before.

I began to call them one by one.

Meg Lindquist was the first.

"Hi, I'm a friend of Clara Parks," I said. "I'm so sorry to tell you that Clara is no longer with us. I wanted to let you know about her memorial service."

Then I shut up and let her talk.

Meg Lindquist was unemotional. "We've heard. Where did you get my number?"

That was my opening. If she didn't even act concerned, it set off a red flag.

"Can you think of anyone who might want her dead?" I said.

"Who did you say this was?"

"A friend. Who is also a private investigator," I said.

"I barely knew her. She was an intern. I work in the executive offices of the Jeffrey Phillips Law Firm. Interns are a dime a dozen."

"Clara Parks wasn't a dime a dozen," I said in a steely voice.

The woman exhaled loudly. "That's not what I meant."

I tried the other names on the list. A few people seemed shocked and shaken by the news. Others were suitably subdued. Nobody was as cold as Meg Lindquist.

Interesting.

I decided to go visit her at home. At night. In the dark.

Danny had given me all the personal details of the employees, including home addresses.

The next morning, I was in front of Meg Lindquist's apartment building at five. I had no idea how early she left for work, and I didn't want to take the chance of missing her.

When I saw the picture Danny had sent over, I realized she was the woman I'd seen leaving the building right when the men in gray suits had arrived. Her title, according to the info Danny had provided, was "executive secretary."

She came out the door at six. She was carrying a garment bag and was dressed in leggings and tennis shoes. A black car pulled up, and she hopped in the back.

I followed her, keeping a few car lengths back. She was dropped off at a gym that was half a block from the law firm's building.

I parked and walked over to the front door. A man was leaving and held the door for me.

I thanked him and smiled.

Inside, I didn't see Meg Lindquist. I followed signs to the

locker room. She wasn't there, either. Then I saw a sign that advertised sunrise rooftop yoga. Boom.

I found the stairs, and sure enough, there were half a dozen people on yoga mats on the roof.

I decided to wait in the locker room.

I hid in a stall until I heard voices.

I peeked out. I could see Meg Lindquist in front of a locker stripping down. Then she grabbed a towel and headed for the showers.

I stepped out of the stall and washed my hands. In the mirror, I watched the other woman grab her bag and leave the locker room.

I decided to have a conversation with Meg when she was at her most vulnerable.

She'd just dropped her towel on the bench in front of her locker when I came up behind her and yanked her arm back, twisting it up against her shoulder blades.

"Jesus!" she cried in pain.

"I don't want to hurt you," I said.

"My purse is in the locker right there. Just take it and leave."

"I don't want your money. I want to know why your boss had Clara killed."

The woman actually scoffed. "Jesus. You again?"

"Yes," I said, tightening my grip on her arm. "Me again."

"Ow. Back off."

"Why? What did Clara do?"

The woman didn't answer.

I twisted harder.

"You're going to break my arm, and I still won't tell you anything."

"That's too bad. It will be hard to type with one arm."

"I don't type, you Neanderthal. I'm the executive assistant not the goddamn secretary."

"I don't care what you do. Just tell me what you know."

"Forget it. Do me a favor and call 911 on your way out so they can come fix my arm after you break it."

I laughed. "If you weren't such a cold bitch, I'd probably like you."

She gave an exaggerated sigh. "I'm going to be late for work. I don't know anything so just let me go."

I let go of her arm.

She rubbed it and gave me an angry look. Then she began to unzip the garment bag, which was hanging on a tall locker. She extracted a silky blouse and put it on without a bra and then tugged on a pair of lace underwear and some soft pants.

"If you don't tell me, you could be considered an accessory to murder," I said.

"Fuck off. My boss is the biggest attorney in town. His brother is the DA. You are a fool to threaten me. Me, of all people."

"Okay," I said. "I'm done playing nice."

I reached into my jacket and took out my phone. I hit Facetime for Danny. He answered immediately. But it wasn't his face on the screen. He was holding up a small white cat. It mewled into the phone's camera.

"Your cat is fucking dead unless you tell me what's going on."

It was all a bluff. It wasn't even her cat.

Danny had mentioned during his sleuthing that Lindquist had a cat that looked exactly like his own.

I'd told him to pretend the cat was his hostage if I Facetimed him.

"Jesus. You're a monster," the woman said and reached wildly for my phone. I hung it up before she could get a good look at the cat.

"Why Clara?"

"I don't know. I swear."

"What *do* you know?"

"I gave her a thick folder to file one day," Meg Lindquist said, eyeing my phone. "And when Jeffrey found out, he lost his shit. He almost fired me. It didn't make sense. It was a standard task for an intern. I'd found the file on his desk and put it on a stack of folders for her to file in the main room. He demanded the file back and then called Clara into his office."

She paused.

"What else?"

"That's it. That's all I can think of."

"Why do you think it's about that file folder?" I asked.

"He fired her the next day."

I nodded.

"One last question," I said. "What was the name on the file folder?"

23

Sutro.

It had taken a second call to Danny for her to give up the name.

When I left the gym, I sat in my Maserati and connected Danny and James in a group text.

"I think Clara was killed because of something she saw in a file folder marked with this name. Does it mean anything to you guys? Can you dig around?"

Then I did the practical thing and googled the name. Huh. An Adolph Sutro was the mayor of San Francisco until 1897.

I'd just finished reading a boring story about him when I looked up and saw Meg Lindquist standing on the sidewalk in front of the gym. She was holding her cell phone and pointing it at me. Taking a picture?

I pulled out of my spot and drove away, but it was too late.

Someone had my license plate number.

I knew enough to not register my car to my home address, but with my license plate information, Phillips would soon know exactly who I was.

Things could get interesting.

Darling and Mrs. Parks had asked me to lunch. Darling was hosting at her place in Marin County. I swung by North Beach first and picked up a decadent meat and cheese platter from my favorite Italian restaurant.

On the drive across the Golden Gate bridge, I dialed Anthony.

"Hey," I said.

"Gia Fucking Santella!" he said with enthusiasm.

"I was just thinking of you," I said.

"Really? I like that."

"I also wanted to run something by you."

"Aha, the real reason you called."

I didn't deny it.

"I think Phillips is a stone cold killer. I think he hired a hitman to kill four young people. But his brother is the DA. As far as I can tell he's untouchable. Do you know him?"

Before Anthony was a state senator, he was mayor of San Francisco.

"Not well," Anthony said. "His brother is a good guy, but that doesn't mean anything."

"How good of a guy?"

"He's a straight up politician as far as I know. I'd say you could trust him."

"Hmmm," I said. "He's made some suspicious accusations disappear."

"Huh," Anthony said.

"I don't have any proof, but I just feel like he's cut from the same cloth as his brother," I said.

"In that case, I'd go with your gut instinct," Anthony said, reminding me of why I liked him so much. "I'll ask around. Discreetly."

"Thanks."

"When am I going to see you next?"

"Soon, I hope."

I was surprised to realize I meant it.

"Let's make it happen," he said. "Listen, I better run. Session is starting."

I was nearly to Darling's when I got an idea. I'd ask Alisha Parks if I could visit Clara's apartment. There might be something there that would help me figure out what she knew that had gotten her killed. Her place had been ransacked for a reason. Maybe the killers found what they'd been looking for. Or maybe they hadn't, and it was still there.

I needed to visit Robert Enzenauer in jail again. He'd probably been the one to search her place.

―――

Lunch with Darling and Alisha Parks was painful.

Both women had dark circles under their eyes.

"We just miss her so much," Mrs. Parks said and then delicately bit into a flaky pastry.

Darling reached over to hold her free hand.

"I'm so sorry."

There was a moment of silence and then Darling cleared her throat.

"We invited you here because the family has decided to go visit Robert Enzenauer in jail and forgive him publicly."

I opened my mouth to speak and then closed it again.

Alisha Parks reached for my hand now. "Gia, I know that it might seem strange to you, but we need to do it to find peace."

I shook my head. "I don't understand, that's all."

"I know," she said. "I used to feel the same way when I was your age."

I tried not to bristle. Instead, I gave a weak smile.

"It's not for him that we are forgiving," she said. "It's for us. It will allow us to move on if we let go of the hate in our hearts."

I perked up a little. At least she was admitting she felt hatred. That made more sense to me.

"I was wondering if it would be possible to visit Clara's apartment?" I asked.

Mrs. Parks frowned.

"I'm hoping to find some evidence that might show why she was killed."

"Well, the police have gone over it very thoroughly," she said.

I nodded. "I'm sure they have, but I have a theory I'd like to explore."

"Gia." Darling's voice held a warning.

"What theory?" Mrs. Parks asked.

"About Jeffrey Phillips's involvement in her death."

"Involvement?" Mrs. Parks asked, looking at Darling. "I don't understand."

"I am not sure her killer acted alone. I can share my theory with you," I said carefully.

Mrs. Parks gave Darling a look.

"Okay," she said.

"I believe he was hired by the attorney who Clara worked for last summer. Where she was an intern."

Mrs. Parks sat back in her chair. Her brow furrowed. "I don't understand."

"I can't prove it yet," I said. "But I believe Clara saw something. Her friends were just part of the cover up, same as the drugs that were planted there."

"Oh no," Mrs. Parks said and put her hands up to her face for a brief second. When she removed them, she looked right at me. "It doesn't end, does it?"

I shook my head.

She rummaged in her handbag and handed me a set of keys.

"You're welcome to go look. I don't think you'll find anything, though."

I nodded. Her faith in the police was absolute. And that was okay.

"Thank you."

Mrs. Park's eyes were wide.

"Please be careful."

"Of course," I said, knowing it was a lie. Darling knew it was too. She gave an exaggerated sigh and shook her head.

"Gia Santella, will you please let the police do their jobs?" she said. "I'm assuming you told James about all of this?"

I nodded.

"Good."

She turned to Mrs. Parks. "We don't want Gia to put herself in danger or do anything to harm this man do we?"

"Oh heavens no!" Mrs. Parks said.

I stood to leave.

Mrs. Parks put her hand on my sleeve.

"Please remember, we don't believe in vengeance or revenge. We believe in forgiveness. If you do find this man guilty, please let the police handle it. The justice system will prevail."

I didn't answer. I wasn't going to make any promises I couldn't keep.

"Gia!" Darling said.

"I'll try," I said as I walked out.

24

When I pulled back onto the road leaving Darling's driveway, there was a small silver sedan parked down the road. I watched it in my rearview mirror, but because of the way the sunlight was hitting the vehicle's windshield, I couldn't tell if there was anyone inside.

I kept my eye on the car as long as I could, but after a turn, I couldn't see it any longer.

I decided to stop in Sausalito for a coffee and to pick up an order of cannoli from a baker there I loved. I'd leave the package in the staff break room at the hotel.

That way I'd also be able to tell if I was being followed.

I took the exit for Sausalito and pulled over to the side of the road.

Nobody followed me.

A few cars did exit after about five minutes, but none of them were silver sedans.

Sausalito was less busy than usual since it was a weekday, but it was still tough finding a place to park.

The streets were filled with tourists.

The line for the town's famous hamburger joint wrapped around the block.

Even though I was full from brunch at Darling's, the smell of frying beef made my mouth water.

I crossed the street and entered my favorite little bakery.

"Ciao," the owner said. I wondered if he recognized me from months back, could tell I was part Italian, or simply greeted everyone that way.

"Ciao," I said, smiling, and then asked for my items in Italian.

He didn't raise an eyebrow. So much for impressing him.

The smells were making me swoon. I watched as an employee put fresh Pizzelle cookies in the case. "How about fifty of those, as well," I said.

He nodded, and the employee stopped what she was doing to head to the back room.

After gathering my order, the owner followed me out to my car, carrying the boxes of goodies. He helped me put them in my trunk and then handed me a small paper bag.

"This will make you the happiest woman on earth," he said and left.

I peeked inside. It was a small flaky pastry that smelled heavenly.

I carried it with me as I walked to the coffee shop. There was no way on earth you could eat something like that without an espresso to accompany it.

I ordered my espresso and a few bags of ground coffee for the breakroom.

Then I sat down and ate the pastry and drank my espresso.

Totally worth the detour to stop in Sausalito. And my employees would be happy.

When I finished, it was time for me to head straight over to the jail for visiting hours. I'd deliver my goodies to the breakroom later, but they'd still be delicious and were packaged well enough to stay fresh.

As I made my way to the Richmond Bridge, I noticed a silver sedan several cars back. Maybe I was paranoid, but maybe not.

I decided to pull over and see what the car did.

As I expected, the driver continued past me without applying the brakes. Just like I would've done. But instead of going straight onto the bridge, the driver took the last exit. Interesting.

I decided to wait out whoever it was, just in case they were following me.

The only thing I was losing was time.

I looked behind me, in case the car had doubled back, and watched the traffic coming toward me. I waited for nearly twenty minutes before I decided to start my engine.

I reached down to check my phone and felt a massive blow as something smashed into my car, sending it flying into oncoming traffic. Luckily, I'd just straightened back up in my seat when the rear end of my car was hit, so my seatbelt locked and jerked me back against the seat. My airbag deployed, and, for a few seconds, all I saw was white dust and felt something firm push me back into the seat. I heard the screech of shuddering brakes and skidding tires and punched down the deflated airbag in time to see a semi heading my way. I watched helplessly. The cab of the truck stopped, but the tractor trailer behind it did what seemed like a slow motion skid around the side of the cab. It was heading right my way. I instinctively threw up my arms and hands to protect myself, knowing deep down inside that it was futile.

To my astonishment, the trailer came to a stop a few feet in front of my hood. Meanwhile, chain reactions were happening everywhere. Cars rear ended others, the air punctuated by the sound of crunching metal and squealing brakes.

Once the sounds stopped, I remembered what had happened and glanced in my rearview mirror. I couldn't tell which vehicle had hit me first. There were five vehicles behind me. They all had damage.

The way behind me was completely blocked by stopped cars and trucks.

People were starting to emerge from their vehicles.

I opened my door and raced over to a car where I saw a dazed woman with blood dripping down her temple.

On my way there, I distinctly heard a car start up and turned to see that silver sedan with its hood completely crunched, heading my way at full speed.

I began to run as it accelerated toward me, sideswiping another car. As it came closer, I saw that the window was open. A black handgun was pointed my way.

I flung myself behind the semi truck's trailer just as the sound of gunshots ripped through the air.

25

Nobody saw the driver of the silver sedan.

Not a soul.

And the police questioned everyone.

The only evidence that I was telling the truth was the two bullets embedded in the side of the semi-truck's trailer.

I was still waiting for James to pick me up when they hoisted my car onto the bed of the tow truck and drove away.

At that point, all the ambulances had left and all but one police vehicle remained.

Nobody, thank God, had life-threatening injuries.

One woman had been taken by ambulance for a broken leg. Another man, who hadn't been wearing his seatbelt, had most likely suffered a concussion. The elderly woman with the cut on her temple had received the wound from the deployment of the airbag.

I had a sore neck.

The EMT who checked me out said I was lucky I was driving a Maserati because it could've been a lot worse.

I agreed that it could've been worse, but I wasn't sure the brand of the car had mattered.

Not to mention, it would have been a lot worse if I hadn't been able to avoid the hail of bullets that were fired at me after the crash.

But I kept that little bit of gratitude to myself.

When James finally pulled up, I had just taken the officer up on his offer to sit in his squad car to stay warm.

The breeze from the bay was tolerable—unless you had been sitting out in it for an hour like me.

We had been making small talk about stupid stuff when the cop said, "I know my investigator already interviewed you, but any reason why someone would ram you like that and then shoot at you?"

He'd been so nice to me—talking about his kids and wife and their upcoming family vacation—that I decided to answer somewhat truthfully.

"You know the old story—powerful but corrupt guy in power tries to take out meddling kids," I glanced over at him. "You're old enough to know Scooby Doo, right?"

He laughed. "If it wasn't for those meddling kids," he recited.

"Well, I'm one of those meddling kids."

He sat there quietly for a minute and then said, "So that's how you know James Hunt?"

"Sort of," I said, trying to evade further questioning. "Do you know him?"

"Just of him. I used to work at the SFPD before I got on with the highway patrol."

"Really?" I asked. "Did you work with him?"

"Nah," he said. "Years after he left. But I respect the hell out of him. Will you tell him?"

I glanced up and saw his Bureau-issue Crown Vic parking.

"You can tell him yourself."

I got out of the squad and stood waiting for James to park and come over to me.

When he got there, he surprised me by wrapping me in a hug.

"Glad you're okay," he said.

"Thanks." Then I remembered. "How's Janie?"

"We'll find out more tomorrow."

"Is she scared?"

He scratched his head. "No. She's fearless."

"I love her," I said.

Then we noticed the state trooper had gotten out of the squad and was rounding the hood of his car. I introduced the two of them. They spoke for a moment and then we got in James's car and left.

"Phillips knows I'm on to him, and he knows who I am," I said and filled James in on my conversation with Meg Lindquist, her snapping photos, and the car following me all the way from Darling's house.

"I wasn't going to say anything, but I hope you didn't tell that trooper much."

"I didn't," I said. "Why?"

"There's a third Phillips brother."

"What?" I said and then realized. "Let me guess. He's a cop?"

"Yeah. That family has all its bases covered. Attorney. DA. Cop."

"Fuck me."

"We just have to be very careful. He is going to come after you, and it could come from any direction," James said, glancing in his rearview mirror.

Then it hit me.

"Shit. If he's on to me, he's going to know about you, and that puts you in danger."

"It'd be pretty ballsy to go after a fed."

"But still."

"I'll be careful."

I shook my head. I was worried.

"I don't want you to drop me off at the hotel in case someone is there waiting for me and sees you."

"Gia…" he began.

"I insist. Besides, I need to stop in North Beach to get some treats for my staff. I promised them cannoli, but I think all of the cannoli's were smashed to shit in the back of my car."

"We'll stop in North Beach, and then I'll drive you to the hotel."

I kept my mouth shut. I wouldn't argue with him. Instead, I'd just do what I wanted once we got to North Beach. Besides, the whole pastry thing was a ruse to get him to drop me off somewhere else. As soon as we stopped in the Italian section, I would take off. I knew that area like the back of my hand, and I'd easily ditch him.

And now that the jail visit wasn't going to happen, I'd decided to go investigate Clara's apartment. I'd lose James and then take a cab to her place.

It was a good plan.

I dozed off during the drive back to the city. Something about the heated seats, soft music, and freeway whirring underneath the Crown Vic's tires put me out.

I woke up when James came to a stop in North Beach.

He'd pulled into a spot near Washington Square Park and St. Patrick's Cathedral.

"I wasn't sure which shop you wanted to go to, but I know this is one of your favorites," he said.

I looked around, blinking. We were closest to Delmonico's. It was one of my favorite spots. But so was the place around the corner, La Bella Rossini. I used to go there with Bobby before he was murdered.

It was at that restaurant that the first attacks had come.

A woman died in my arms after a car plowed into the restaurant in an attempt to run me down. That woman had been the sister of an enemy I didn't even know I had. That enemy had then murdered Bobby and Matt—Dante's new husband—just hours after their wedding.

North Beach was ripe with ghosts and vivid memories of people I had loved.

And yet I still adored the area.

"This is the closest spot I could find."

"Perfect," I said with a smile and got out.

26

I made the mistake of stopping to wave at James before I entered the restaurant.

Shit.

He'd be suspicious now.

I was counting on him not knowing that there was another door to the restaurant around the corner. I walked in and then straight through the restaurant to the other door. I was back out on the sidewalk around the corner, out of sight, and hailing a cab within five minutes.

I didn't feel an ounce of guilt. I told him no and he'd insisted, so it was his own damn fault.

Plus, I knew he'd secretly admire that I'd outmaneuvered him.

I told the cab driver to drop me off at an intersection close to Clara's building.

When the driver pulled onto Clara's street, I told him to circle the block once very slowly. As he did, I glanced in all the parked cars looking for anyone—cop or killer—who might be staking out the place. All the cars were empty, so I told the driver to pull over and let me out a few doors down. I paid him and got out and then started walking in the opposite direction. I didn't want anyone to know where I was going.

Once the cab had turned a corner, I waited to the count of ten and then turned around. I let myself into the lobby and held the door as it closed so it wouldn't make any noise. I saw from the mailboxes that Clara's apartment was on the third floor. I crept up the old wooden stairs, trying not to make any sounds. I waited at the third floor landing, listening for any indication that someone had heard me. When I didn't hear anything, I opened her door, slipped in, and closed it as quietly as possible. I locked it behind me and flicked on the flashlight on my phone. I was relieved to see blackout curtains, so I yanked those closed and turned on a tableside lamp.

The place felt like a furnace. The heat had been cranked up. It was nearly unbearable. I thought about trying to find a thermostat but figured I wouldn't be inside long enough for it to matter.

I remembered that Darling had said the place had been ransacked.

Drawers were pulled out and emptied. Every cupboard was open.

The place was trashed. The girl obviously hadn't been a hoarder. The biggest mess was from books and papers on the ground.

And the detectives had probably made it worse. At the very least, investigators had left fingerprint dust over everything. I was sure Enzenauer had broken in and so, of course, his fingerprints in her apartment would have sealed his case even without the confession.

I wondered if Clara's family was going to clean the place out. It seemed wrong to just leave it abandoned like it was.

"I'm at Clara's," I texted Darling. "Is there anything her mom wants?"

I eyed the full closet and framed photos and knickknacks.

A few seconds later, Darling replied.

"Photos. Perfume. Antique hairbrush. Thanks."

I looked under the sink and found a plastic garbage bag. I filled it with the items Darling had mentioned and then began to look around more carefully.

It was clear that Clara hadn't owned much and was a minimalist. I could see why Mrs. Parks hadn't already been there. There wasn't a whole lot of belongings left besides all the books and papers. The top of a small desk was empty.

The investigators had taken her laptop, which was unfortunate because that surely had some interesting info on it.

I stood back and glanced at the room. Where would someone hide something of value or import? I remembered that the women at Darling's party had been telling that funny story about the scorned ex-wife putting stinky cheese in the tubular curtain rods. I remembered that Clara had laughed especially loud.

It was a gamble, since she'd probably only come home to change after the party before heading out that night to the club where the killer had found her.

But it was worth a shot. I was starting to sweat, so I took off my motorcycle jacket and hung it on the back of a kitchen chair.

I grabbed another chair and pulled it over to the curtains over the window facing away from the street. I peeked out quickly and saw that the window faced another building without windows. Perfect.

I lifted the curtain rod off its hook and then set the rod with the curtains still attached on the kitchen table. My heart raced when I heard something sliding around inside the circular curtain tube. I unscrewed the small decorative knob and tilted it toward the ground. A thumb drive slid out and landed on the rug below.

Holy shit.

I scooped up the thumb drive and put the curtain rod back up, straightening the curtains. I noticed the top half of the window had slipped open a few inches, and there wasn't a screen. I was lifting the window to close it when I heard a sound in the room behind me. I had the thumb drive clutched in my palm.

"Freeze! Put your hands up where I can see them." Right then, my hands were about chest level at the open window. My body would hide what I was about to do. Very slowly, I stuck my right hand out the window and released the thumb drive into the darkness below.

Then I stuck both hands straight up.

"Very carefully get down from the chair."

I did, keeping my balance as I stepped down.

The voice wasn't familiar.

"Now turn around slowly."

I did.

A man stood there, pointing a gun at me.

He looked like a crankster. He had pale, pockmarked skin and was emaciated. His hair was greasy and lanky. Then it struck me why he looked familiar.

"You're Robert Enzenauer's brother, Donald, aren't you? You're the one who helped kill those kids."

"Aren't you a fucking rocket scientist?" he said.

"Were you the one in the silver car?" I asked. I knew he was. I was stalling, my eyes searching the room for a weapon.

My gun was in my leather motorcycle jacket on the chair by the door.

"Enough questions," he said. "You're wanted elsewhere."

"Let me just grab my coat," I said casually.

He looked at where I pointed.

He backed up, picked up my coat, and patted the pockets without lowering the gun he had pointed at me.

"Lookie what we have here," he said, taking out my gun. He stuck it in his back waistband.

If I could get within striking range of him, I could take him out.

He was a skinny, weak drug addict.

But he was also dangerous. Because he was a skinny, weak drug addict.

He would probably shoot me without blinking. He opened the door.

"You first. Don't try any funny business. I'm supposed to bring you alive, but he didn't say anything about you being in one piece. I'm an ex-Marine. I can shoot your kneecap off at thirty yards."

Fuck. He wasn't just a junkie.

I'd have to go along with him. For now.

And it might work out in my favor. The person he referred to as "he" had to be Phillips.

I would be led right to the lion's den.

It hadn't been my first plan, but I was willing to adapt.

I walked out the door and felt the gun in my side.

"I can shoot you right here, and you'll still live long enough for me to deliver you, you got it?" he hissed in my ear.

"Got it."

Downstairs there was a four-door, piece-of-shit sedan idling in the middle of the street.

"You're driving."

He crawled in the backseat at the same time I got into the driver's seat.

Before he could say a word, I stepped on the gas as hard as I could.

He swore and the gun fired. Since I hadn't been hit, I kept going, driving like a fucking mad woman through the streets of San Francisco, taking the corners like a banshee. Then, out of nowhere, a car appeared in front of me. I saw a frightened face look at me, lit up by my headlights. I slammed on the brakes and came to a skidding halt inches away from their driver's side door.

I barely had time to breathe a sigh of relief before something hit my temple, and the world went black.

27

I woke in darkness.

My hands were bound behind my back. My face pressed into something gritty that smelled like dirt.

I involuntarily groaned, and I felt a boot on my back pressing me harder into the ground.

"Stay put, princess," a voice said. I heard the flick of a lighter.

"I can't breathe," I said, relieved that my mouth wasn't gagged.

The man let out a cackle.

"Just wait," he said. "I'm having a smoke even though he told me not to. You won't tell, will you?"

It was the man from the apartment. I recognized his voice.

"Why didn't he want you to smoke?"

I was suddenly concerned about an explosion.

"No reason. Just to be a dickhead."

I rolled over, expecting a boot to the rib cage, but it sounded like the man was too busy rustling a cigarette out of a pack.

"What did you mean when you said 'just wait?'"

"When high tide comes in, you're fucked."

That was the first clue as to where I'd been taken, but it still didn't add up. I didn't doubt for a second there were tunnels along the coast that filled with water during high tide. But it didn't tell me where we were.

"Why is it so dark in here?"

"Dunno. Boss man said to keep the lights off until he arrives above."

Above. I lodged that small detail, as well.

Suddenly, blinding lights flicked on.

"Fuck!" the junkie said and dropped his cigarette near my head. He stepped on it with his scuffed boot.

I heard the sound of feet on the stairs. Several feet and low voices. The noises were all coming from behind me.

I glanced around. We were inside a cave. The walls were lined with jagged outcroppings of rocks. The cave narrowed past my feet, and I saw a black hole at the end and could hear the distant sounds of the ocean. Behind me, the cave was bigger, and there was a large steel door.

The door swung open and Phillips stood there surrounded by four men in gray suits.

Probably the same ones I'd seen enter his law firm.

"Gentlemen, I'm glad you could all be here today. Along with your first official tour, I wanted you to see for yourself that our little problem is being taken care of."

There were low chuckles.

Tour of what? This cave?

"Hey, fuckwad," I said. "Why don't you let me go before all of you wind up in prison for kidnapping."

Before I realized it, he'd fired a gun that kicked up the dirt near my head.

"Recognize this little piece?" he said. "It's your own gun."

I squinted. He was holding my Glock 26. They'd taken it from my jacket. It only had four rounds in it. Now that he'd fired it, there were three.

I was going to get him to fire again. He probably assumed it had a full ten rounds in the clip.

"Fuck you!" I screamed. He fired again. My heart raced as the bullet struck the wall opposite us. That shot was even further away. I was counting on him being too much of a wuss to actually kill me. But I probably shouldn't have counted on him being a *good* shot. A sloppy shot could kill me. Two rounds left.

"This is fun," he said and then, idiot that he was, he fired another round toward the empty black hole leading to the ocean.

My kidnapper leaned over and whispered something to him. Probably about what a dumbass he was to waste rounds. Phillips tucked the gun away and smiled at his guests.

"Meg is almost here," he said. "I'm going to let her show you around while I have a little chat with our guest. See that plank of wood right there? I've had special braces installed on it. This woman's wrists will be locked to the plank, and when the tide comes in, sayonara. We'll come back tomorrow when the tide goes out again, so you can see what happens to people who oppose us."

I strained to see the plank, but it was at the far end of the tunnel.

"I'm going to film the whole thing so we can use it as a warning."

Then I heard the click-clacking of high heels.

"Aw, here Meg is now."

I looked up to see the executive assistant come off the staircase and walk straight toward me. She crouched down, and before I could react, slapped me across the face.

"Strip her down," she said as she stood. "She wanted to play when I was naked and vulnerable; let's see how she likes it."

Fuck. But her words were ignored.

"Gentleman, follow Meg, she will show you the rest of the facility."

I heard them all leave.

"Jasper," he said. "You go on. Leave us alone."

"Yes, sir."

"I won't be needing your services for the rest of the night."

"Yes, sir."

"Close that steel door behind us."

"What if it locks and traps you in here with her?" he said. "You told me not to close that door or I'd get locked in."

"You numbskull. I have a key. Just close the damn door."

I heard it slam shut.

"Where am I?" I asked.

"If you don't know, I guess you weren't as big a threat as I thought," he said and laughed.

I didn't respond.

"We are in the bowels of a secret coal mine. We are two hundred feet down the cliff from Deadman's Point."

Holy shit. We were still in the city. I could've sworn we were somewhere remote on the coast of California. We were in San Francisco, at Land's End near Sea Cliff where Phillips had his house.

"We are just above a coal vein that will make me the richest man on the planet."

"I thought coal mining was déclassé."

"Ha!" he laughed. "Didn't you hear? It's coming back with a vengeance. And I have spent the past five years developing this mine and buying up all the surrounding property."

"Goodie for you," I said and struggled to sit up.

He didn't stop me. He was too busy climbing a ladder

propped against a nearby wall. Near the top there was a small platform on a ledge that held a video camera.

"We're just going to turn this baby on and then I'm going to get you all strapped in, sweetheart."

I was up and running toward the ladder before the words finished coming out of his mouth. I threw my entire torso into the base of the ladder, and it began to wobble. I pushed harder and it started to tip. Phillips screamed and tumbled from the rung he was standing on. I ducked right before he landed on me. He crashed onto his back with a loud thud. I heard him groan and knew he probably was only knocked out. Meanwhile, I began to rub the binding securing my wrists on the sharp outcropping of rocks I'd spotted earlier.

I worked the cloth over the sharp stones past Phillips, who was still moaning and twitching every once in a while. As soon as I cut through the cloth, I raced over to Phillips and searched his pockets. Inside his coat was a set of keys. My hands were shaking as I tried the first key in the door while keeping an eye on Phillips, expecting him to rise from the ground like Freddy Krueger. I needed to get out before Meg returned or Phillips woke up. I tried three keys before I found the right one. I opened it and immediately shut it behind me.

A small part of me remembered that Mrs. Parks hadn't wanted Clara's killer dead. I'd get out of this hell hole and call the police. They could find him here. If he was lucky, they'd come before high tide.

On the other side of the door was a steep staircase. The ceiling and walls were polished steel. Very interesting. Doors were scattered along the way, but I wanted to get to the top and get out. I raced up the stairs until it felt like I'd run a marathon. At the top, was another door, this one without a lock. I swung it open and stepped inside.

I was in a high-tech command center with monitors showing

cameras positioned through the coal mines. There was another door on the other side that said "Exit." Bingo.

As I made my way across the room, I looked at the monitors. The place had cameras everywhere. One camera showed the deep cavern I'd been in. I saw the ladder on the ground. I saw the wooden plank with the steel cuffs. And I saw that the rest of the room was empty. *Fuck.*

I heard a sound behind me. I turned and Phillips was there. He had a gun. My gun.

He pointed it at me, and I knew it was over.

But…Phillips had fired all but one round.

I shouted and lunged behind a bank of desks just as he fired.

He missed. Game over.

I raced for the exit. I burst through the door and into the night air.

I'd only gone about ten feet when something slammed into me and knocked me to the ground.

28

THE SOUND OF SIRENS AND FLASHING LIGHTS FILLED THE AIR.

The person who had tackled me was gone. I heard shouting and footsteps running away.

"San Francisco police!"

I stood and held my hands up. To my surprise, Phillips was beside me with his hands up, as well.

"Officer, I think there must be a misunderstanding. I'm the owner of this property. I just found a trespasser here and called all of you. May I put my hands down?"

"Who are you?"

"My name is Jeffrey Phillips."

There was some mumbling and then the officer said, "Come on over here so we can clear this up. You say this woman was trespassing?"

"Yes, sir."

"That's bullshit," I said. "He kidnapped me and brought me here to kill me."

"Those are some pretty serious charges, missy," he said. "I'd hate to see you also charged with libel along with trespassing."

"Put your hands behind your back."

I did as I was told. I was tempted to tell them to call James, but I didn't dare say his name in front of Phillips.

I was stuffed in the back of the squad car and taken to the station. Phillips leaned into the door of the squad car before it closed and said, "I'm not done with you."

Once we arrived at the station, I was about to ask for my one phone call when I saw James enter my holding cell.

"She's been accused of federal crimes," he said. "We're taking custody of her right now."

It was only when I was safely in his Crown Vic that he said, "Jesus, Gia. It's a good thing you were wearing your necklace."

"What?"

"Your necklace."

"Huh?" He was pointing to the necklace that Anthony had given to me.

"Don't hate me," he said.

I reached up to touch the necklace. "What are you talking about?"

My voice was shrill.

"It has a tracker in it."

I didn't know what to be more angry about. The fact that James was tracking my movements with a fucking necklace or that he had somehow conned my latest lover into tricking me into wearing it.

"I'm furious."

"It just saved your life."

"Maybe. Maybe not." I crossed my arms.

"Let's go."

I pretended I was sleepy the whole way home, yawning repeatedly.

When he pulled in front of the hotel, I gave an extra exaggerated yawn.

"Thanks, James."

"You know, if you hadn't ditched me in North Beach, you wouldn't have been in this situation."

"If you were following me, what took you so damn long to find me?"

"I let you go, Gia. I wasn't worried about you until both Anthony and Dante called and said they couldn't reach you. That's when I remembered the tracker."

"Wait? You forgot about it until then?"

"I swear," he said. "I got a lot on my mind."

"Oh shit. Janie?"

"We don't know anything yet."

"I'm sorry."

"Get some sleep," he said.

I leaned over and kissed his cheek.

"Thanks for saving me," I said.

I walked inside and then hid behind a large column until I saw his taillights disappear down the road. Then I went back out and hailed a cab.

I was outside Clara's apartment within fifteen minutes. I crept around the back of the building and came across a metal gate. The space between the two buildings was basically a small empty lot with overgrown weeds. I picked the lock and was inside searching the ground with the flashlight on my phone. A few seconds later, I had the thumb drive. Thank God it was intact.

Then I was back at my hotel, sticking the thumb drive into my laptop.

A file came up with photos.

Sutro's Coal Mine. Sutro. The name on the file folder.

Bingo.

Some were pictures of the mine and maps. Other pictures were snapshots of documents.

A few documents were titles showing that Phillips owned the property.

But if Phillips owned the land, I wasn't sure what Clara could have seen that made him kill her and her friends.

I looked at the documents and photos again.

There were two different documents that seemed almost identical. I zoomed in and that's when I realized what I was looking at. Thousands of lives were in danger.

Clara must have threatened to expose him.

There were two environmental impact reports for the coal mining project, both dated the same day. But there were key differences in each one, and they had been drawn up by two different inspectors.

The first report was written by an environmental scientist.

His report and statement said that the impact of the coal mining operation would pollute the water of San Francisco enough to likely cause birth defects and cancer. The inspector said that even though the levels might technically be under EPA standards, the project should be shut down because people would surely become ill and die. He cited other cities around the world with the same levels of toxins in their water and the increased incidence of cancer and birth defects.

The report said that early testing showed that the water coming out of the coal mine contained arsenic, copper, lead, and mercury, and the burn-off of coal creates mercury that ends up in the water and then in the fish people eat. If they weren't drinking the toxins, they might be eating it. The inspector wrote that, once upon a time, the EPA had protections in place to prevent this sort of contamination, but recent administrations had rolled back these protections.

The second report simply stated that the toxin levels were within acceptable EPA standards.

I typed in the name of the inspector who wrote the "everything-is-hunky-dory" report.

He wasn't a scientist. He was an attorney specializing in environmental law. He also came up as a Stanford grad. Like Phillips. I looked at the years he was in school. The two men had been there the same years. Possibly a crony? Then I looked up the name of the environmental scientist.

The first thing that popped up was a newspaper article stating he was missing.

His family had reported him missing and then a few days later, authorities found his car parked alongside a cliff in Marin, a spot known for suicides. His body had never been found.

It was clear what was going on and what Clara had realized: Phillips had made the original inspector disappear and brought in his own to hide the true dangers of the coal mine's operation.

Which meant people were going to become ill and die.

And it would technically be legal.

In a city like San Francisco, however, the power of protesters could shut down his new company in the blink of an eye. He knew that. And that's why Phillips made sure the report would never see the light of day.

I called him at the law firm. Of course he didn't pick up, so I left a message.

"Gia Santella here."

He called back immediately.

"I have something you want."

"What do you want for it?"

"One hundred K," I said.

"You're crazy."

I tried not to laugh. That much money was pocket change to both of us, but he didn't know that.

"Be ready to hand over the money in two hours. I'll tell you the location. Be ready to meet me. Alone. With the cash."

I hung up.

The next thing I did was google the highest structure in the east bay. I wanted to see him coming and make sure he was alone.

I laughed when I saw what came up.

A fucking roller coaster.

At an amusement park.

The park was closed for the winter.

Perfect.

I dressed in a black shirt, black jeans, my boots, and strapped on a holster that would hold my gun and two of my daggers. I put on my motorcycle jacket. At the last second, I ripped the cornicello necklace off and threw it on my bathroom counter.

What I really needed was a way to record Phillips confessing. I would just have to use my phone and hope it worked. I'd get set up before he arrived and then, once I had the confession and Phillips at gunpoint, I'd call James and have him do the right thing.

Right by Mrs. Parks.

I'd still prefer Phillips dead for killing Clara.

But it wasn't up to me.

I took the emergency service elevator to the top of the roller coaster and then called Phillips.

I'd had him wait a few miles away, telling him I'd call with further instructions.

"The gate to the amusement park is open. Park at the entrance and walk in. I'll call you when I see you are alone.

Ten minutes later, his car pulled in. He got out and began walking into the park. I called him.

"Keep walking toward the roller coaster. I'll be watching you, so don't fuck around. Take the elevator to the top. I'll be waiting."

I hung up and watched him as he grew closer. He called the

elevator down, and I waited until it was nearly to the top before I turned off the ringer on my phone, hit record, and set it on a crossbeam nearby. Then, right before the elevator door opened up, I had a change of heart. I turned the volume all the way down and dialed James's phone number.

Phillips stepped out of the elevator pointing a gun at me. Which was fine because I was pointing a gun back at him.

"I'm pretty sure I'm a faster draw than you," I said.

"Guess we're going to find out."

29

"First, let's talk business," I said. "There's your thumb drive with all your dirty business on it."

"It's not dirty."

"Well, whatever is on there was dirty enough for you to kill Clara and her friends."

"You really don't know what's on the drive?"

I kept my mouth shut. I wanted to hear him say it.

"Did Clara know?" I asked. "Is that why you had her murdered?"

"She knew exactly what she was looking at. She must be a hell of a lot smarter than you are."

"Definitely," I said and shrugged. "She *was* a hell of a lot smarter than me. And she was going to do big things. You are a piece of shit who robbed the world of her bright mind."

"She was threatening to expose the truth."

"Yes, she was," I said. "The truth is, your operation would end up polluting the San Francisco water supply and cause everything from birth defects to cancer. And you're okay with that?"

"Yes. We don't drink water out of the tap."

"But other people do. People who can't afford to buy bottled water. New moms who are struggling and use tap water for their baby's bottles. Hard-working men who fill their thermoses with coffee made from tap water to drink while they are working construction all day. School kids who fill their water bottles to bring to school."

"She was going to turn the original environmental impact report over to the authorities. And even my hotshot brother wouldn't have been able to save me. The whole deal would've fallen through, and the world would be out their next billionaire."

"I think you're mistaken that your coal mine would make you a billionaire, and I think you're a monster to think that it's worth murdering four people."

"It was worth it. Just like your death will be worth it."

"Hear that, James?" I said and looked at the phone propped above his head. "This piece of shit is spilling everything."

Phillips reeled back and looked up at the phone. In one fluid motion, he reached up, plucked my phone from the rail, and chucked it off the side of the roller coaster.

"James is an FBI agent in case you were wondering who I was speaking to."

"I was considering letting you live," he said.

"Excuse me?"

He took a step closer.

"I can't let you live now."

"Back up," I said. "Don't threaten me. We all know your threats are empty anyway. You always have someone else do your dirty work."

"Not this time," he said.

We were more than 400 feet up in the air, balanced on a rickety metal platform on top of the highest roller coaster I'd ever seen.

His dark form remained a silhouette as he grew closer, the hem of his trench coat flapping in the wind behind him. We were so high up I could see the Golden Gate Bridge across the Bay glowing in the night sky behind him.

The wind whipped up a small maelstrom, sending long strands of my hair in front of my eyes, but I ignored it, keeping both arms straight in front of me, both hands wrapped around the Glock 26 that I had pointed at his chest.

It took everything I had not to squeeze the trigger.

I'm not supposed to kill him.

An image of god-fearing women in high-heeled pumps and gloves kneeling in church came back to me.

They were all praying for the soul of this piece of shit who was close enough now that I could kill him easily with one shot. But I held back.

I'd promised Darling I would try not to kill him.

I like to keep my promises.

But damn it. He was making that really hard.

I was shivering even though I had on my thick leather motorcycle jacket.

I crept even closer. That's when he stepped out of the shadow into the light, and I nearly squeezed the trigger right then. He was holding a gun.

It was pointed at me.

"Put the gun down," I yelled. "I told you I'm a better shot. Don't make me prove it."

He was a bit unsteady on his feet, and the barrel of the gun wobbled around a bit. He probably couldn't hit me, but I didn't want to take any chances.

He took a step forward.

"Whoa!" I said and backed up. "Tell me right now why I shouldn't kill you. Put down the gun, or I'll be forced to. And believe me, I *want* to do it."

"I'm not going to prison," he said.

In the distance, I heard the first wail of sirens. Out of my peripheral vision far below me, I saw a line of squad cars with their lights on coming down the freeway toward the amusement park.

I exhaled loudly and tried to control the urge to take Phillips's head off right then and there.

"Listen you piece of shit," I said. "I want you dead. People like you who prey on the weak and helpless, you don't deserve to live. You have destroyed entire families. As far as I can see—and I've looked—you don't have any redeeming qualities."

"Fuck you, you dyke bitch."

I actually laughed out loud.

"That the best you got?" I asked.

He was trembling with rage. Sweat poured down his brow.

In the green and blue lights from the ride, he didn't look so fucking powerful now.

He was no longer the man who made people cower when he barked orders at a restaurant and berated anyone and everyone. He was no longer the boss who slipped his hand up his secretary's skirts and threatened to fire them if they didn't put up with it. He was no longer the cheating husband who flaunted his mistresses and endless string of prostitutes in front of his long-suffering wife.

He was no longer the man who had coldly ordered four murders that had devastated four families.

Nope. He was no longer any of those things.

He looked like a desperate, scared, and pathetic little man.

Which is exactly what he was.

"Time's almost up for you," I said.

My finger was twitching—eager to squeeze the trigger and end the life of this waste of sperm.

But I'd made a promise.

"I said I'm not going to prison."

"You are," I said in a matter-of-fact voice. "It won't be so bad in prison."

"You are going to die," he said. The barrel of his gun wobbled around wildly. I stayed in my stance, trying to keep my weary arms steady.

The sirens were getting closer now. Out of the corner of my eye, I saw the line of cars pull into the amusement park's far entrance.

"You really think you are superior to everyone else, don't you?" I asked. I was genuinely curious. "And you really think you are invincible?"

"I am." His voice was smug. I could blow his fucking head off in two seconds, and yet he was still cocky as fuck.

The squads had stopped below the base of the roller coaster.

I heard the hum of the elevator to our left being summoned.

"They'll be up here in minutes."

"It will be too late," he said.

He gave a blood-curdling primal scream as he pulled the trigger.

But I was faster. I saw his fingers begin to curl before they squeezed the trigger.

My bullet struck him right between the eyes. Right where I aimed it.

He was dead before his body hit the ground.

"God damn it."

I really had tried not to kill him.

I would swear on it.

30

The first officers to arrive on the scene didn't see it that way.

When I stepped out of the elevator on the ground below the roller coaster, I was greeted by half a dozen cops standing in a semicircle, pointing their weapons at me.

"Freeze!" one guy shouted.

I refrained from rolling my eyes at him. I already had my hands in the air.

I mean, duh. The second I saw them, my hands were thrust up above me. I'd seen too many instances where people had been shot by scared or amped up cops.

I tried not to look at the remains of Phillips.

It was not pretty. You fall from the highest structure in the East Bay, you aren't going to be able to have an open casket.

The cops were rushing to get to me, so I said, "I have a gun. It's in a holster on my back. I also have two daggers."

That honesty got me thrown to the ground after they relieved me of my weapons.

They yanked my arms behind my back and cuffed me.

It was all standard procedure, until a guy "accidentally" kicked me in the rib cage as everyone else was walking away.

I grunted involuntarily but didn't react.

I knew that there were still some cops out there loyal to Phillips and his family, and I was making damn sure that I didn't give anyone a reason to shoot me.

But inside I was seething.

The cops were standing around like fuckwads, taking pictures of Phillips body on their cell phones and making comments like "Holy shit. His head looks like a fucking cracked egg."

"Yeah, if an egg had blood and brains in it instead of a yolk."

"I never saw anything that gross in my whole life."

"What about the guy whose head was rolled over by the tractor?"

"Yeah, that was pretty sick."

Another guy was over to the side, vomiting.

That made them all laugh.

I was getting tired of their gallows humor when I heard a car come to a screeching stop nearby.

"Get her off the ground you dumb fucks."

James.

Thank god.

"She's the victim here."

"Then why is there a dead body splattered all over the pavement?"

I turned my head. It was the same cop who'd kicked me— a short fuck with bulging muscles and a crew cut. He had a large nose and thick eyebrows, and I knew he pulled women over like nobody's business. I wanted to poke his eyes out.

Someone yanked me up by my arms and then the cuffs were removed.

I walked straight over to the cop. I got in his face.

"You kick all the girls in your custody in the ribs, or am I special?"

He looked at me like he wanted to smash my teeth in. I knew how he felt.

"What is she talking about?" a voice said.

I turned. It was a sergeant. Oh good, a real man on the scene.

"Listen, Sarge, I'm not going to file a complaint if you let me get one good punch in."

"What? You're fucking nuts," the cop said and spit on the ground.

That's when I saw James for the first time. He had his arms folded across his chest, grinning.

"Go for it," the sergeant said. "Edwards, you flinch, you're on desk duty."

"Fuck."

All the other cops gathered in a semicircle.

This was going to be fun.

Then when he saw all the other cops were watching, he sneered at me. "Give it your best shot. I've taken bigger shits than you."

Before he finished speaking, I had executed a perfect palm strike to his nose.

He reeled back as blood began pouring out of it. He cupped it in both palms.

"Jesus Christ, she broke my fucking nose."

I looked at James.

"Are we done here?"

He nodded.

By the time I had told my story about what happened another half dozen times to the assistant DA, the FBI field office supervisor, the San Francisco Police Chief, and the city's homicide commander, it was early morning.

We had turned over the thumb drive, the confession that James had recorded, and more.

Detectives had been at the jail all night with a district attorney working on a plea agreement for Robert Ebenezeur. If he confessed that he'd been hired by Phillips to kill the four people, he'd have a shot at negotiating prison time somewhere nearby so his daughter could visit him.

James updated me as he drove me back to the hotel.

"He says he'll only take the plea if there is a guarantee he'll be permanently housed at San Quentin. Says he needs to be in the area so his wife and kid can visit him easily."

"Makes sense to me."

"Hey! While you were out solving crime, Janie got the results of her biopsy back."

I could tell from his voice it was good news.

"And?"

"Benign."

"Thank fucking God."

"Right?" James said and punched the steering wheel.

Then he began sobbing. He kept his eyes on the road ahead.

I reached over and squeezed his shoulder.

We didn't say a word the rest of the drive.

EPILOGUE

I slept in until three the next afternoon.

When I woke, I saw that Darling had called.

I was excited to call her.

"You must've heard, " I said as I put a kettle on the stove to make a press pot of coffee.

"Mmmhmm. First, I'm so glad you're okay."

"Who called you?"

"I called James after I couldn't reach you and saw it on the news."

"It's on the news?" I reached for my remote control and flicked on the TV. I scrolled through the local news channels and saw it was on every station. Then I went to the BBC and CNN. All of them. Holy shit. And the ticker at the bottom said the DA was being investigated because he apparently had knowledge of the Sutro deal and had been an investor, along with four men from North Korea. So that's who the men in the gray suits were.

The family of the missing inspector was being interviewed, saying they believed he was murdered. That he had mentioned a client who was dangerous.

"Whoa," I said. "I just woke up. I've got the TV on now. What a shitshow."

"Mmmhmm."

Something about the way she said it set off small alarms.

"What aren't you telling me?" I asked.

"I heard about it because Alisha called me at five in the morning."

"Oh yeah?" I asked warily.

"She's upset."

"Why?" But I knew why. Phillips was dead. She'd made it clear that she didn't want anybody else dead. Not even her daughter's murderer.

"Did you say that I probably had a good reason to kill the guy if I went against her wishes?"

Darling didn't answer.

"Did you? I mean you defended me, right?" I was starting to get angry. "I mean I'm sure you told her that Gia wouldn't kill someone unless she had no other choice. Right? Right, Darling?"

"Gia..." she trailed off without answering.

I held the phone away from me and stared at it. Then, as I felt hot tears form, I hung up.

It took everything I had not to chuck my phone across the room.

What the fuck?

What utter bullshit.

I guess I wasn't completely surprised that Mrs. Parks was disappointed in the outcome, but to have Darling refuse to even defend me? It hurt.

My phone rang.

Darling.

I turned the ringer off.

Epilogue

My kettle was whistling and steam was pouring out. I made a French Press pot of coffee and then added a hefty amount of Bailey's Irish cream to it before taking it out on the deck.

It was a shitty day in the city.

It was cold and windy and gray.

I took out my phone and clicked on the airline's website. Within ten minutes, I'd booked a trip to Cabo San Lucas. I'd be leaving that night.

I texted Eva. "Is the Cabo house available?"

"Yes!" she wrote back. "So happy you're going on a vacation. Enjoy. Love you."

I just hearted her message. I was too deflated to respond.

I thought I'd done the right thing by trying to stop Phillips and had proven he was the killer, so why did I feel like such a loser?

Then I remembered I was supposed to meet up with Anthony while he was in town this weekend. I quickly texted him. "Sorry. Something came up. I miss you." I hit send and then remembered I was also supposed to be pissed about the necklace.

"And if you ever conspire with James or anyone else to track me again, I'm going to kick your ass. Your necklace is going to be ground up and put in your drink the next time you visit."

I hit send.

Maybe it was a little harsh, but I was pissed.

My phone dinged.

"Sorry."

Sorry? That's it? Sorry.

I was angrier than ever.

But I knew that my anger was really all about how hurt I felt by Mrs. Parks and Darling's reaction to what had happened.

Speaking of the devil, Darling called again.

I turned my phone off completely. I needed to pack.

I kept drinking on the flight to Cabo, so I might or might not have been three sheets to the wind when I arrived. Luckily, Eva had arranged for a driver to pick me up. Don't ask me how the woman knew what time I was coming in. She was uncanny like that. Or maybe just a really good fucking hacker who was nosy about her niece's movements. I was okay with that. It wasn't like she put a tracker in a gift she gave me.

The driver waited until I was safely in the gated compound of the house before leaving. I appreciated that and used my app to tip him an extra $100. Good drivers were hard to find.

I let myself into the house, set all the alarms again, and then fell onto the bed in the master suite and was instantly asleep.

I woke in the morning feeling like shit, still dressed in my clothes from the night before.

I looked at myself in the mirror. I looked just like I felt. It was not a good look for me. I was getting too old to do that kind of shit.

I closed my eyes, gripping the sink with both hands.

Get your shit together, Gia.

I stripped down and took a shower, washing away all the grime, but all the pity I'd been feeling for myself the past twelve hours wouldn't scrub off.

When I stepped out, I padded naked through the house and downstairs where I made a green smoothie with fresh spinach, pineapple, blueberries, and strawberries.

Because of course as soon as Eva heard I was coming, she'd had groceries delivered. God bless her.

Then I threw on a one-piece swimsuit and did laps in the pool until I was exhausted. By the time I pulled myself out of the pool, my legs and arms were Jello.

I then drank three glasses of water and ate some sushi I found in the refrigerator.

Wrapped in a cover-up, I perused Eva's impressive bookshelf and plucked a book with an interesting cover and name, *The Elegance of the Hedgehog*. Then I cranked up the outdoor stereo system to play my favorite female rappers—Cardi B, Sawatee, Doja Cat, and headed out to the pool. The compound was surrounded by a stone wall that was taller than the second floor of the house. It afforded utter privacy. The backyard was a tropical garden with a lap pool, a Jacuzzi, an outdoor pizza oven and a full outdoor kitchen. I loved it here.

I took out my leather-bound journal and began to write about my feelings. It was something that I'd only started to do in the past few months. Anthony had mentioned that he did this and thought it might be beneficial to me to sort through some of my, uh, more passionate emotions.

I'd done it halfheartedly since he mentioned it, but found that sitting under the Mexican sun brought a flood of thoughts that I put on paper with ink. Then, to go with it, I traded in my fiction book and found some inspiring nonfiction books in Eva's library.

I placed a stack by my deck chair: Sun Tzu's *The Art of War* (re-reading this one); *The Prince* by Machiavelli; *Six Secret Teachings* by Jiang Ziya; and just to offset the hardcore military strategy books—*The Art of Seduction* by Robert Greene.

I read by the pool until dark, only getting up to replenish my water and nibble on some of the healthy snacks that Eva had stocked—nuts, dried fruit, fresh fruit, vegetables on a platter with dip.

Then, as the rest of the neighborhood awoke from their siestas and began to blare their god awful music and party, I closed myself in the master bedroom, turned up the white noise machine and slept.

I repeated this same pattern for three days until I was detoxed both physically and mentally.

Then I dialed Darling.

"Hey," I said.

"Gia," Darling said and then cut to the chase. "I know you're sad that Alisha is upset. You have to understand that she's having a hard time accepting that Clara's death led to another murder."

"Well, Clara's death almost led to my murder."

"I get that. And I know you don't believe it, but Alisha gets it, as well. It's just going to take her some time to understand. It's all too much."

"Whatever," I said. "I just don't get how her God forgives two men who murdered four young people, but Mrs. Parks doesn't think he would forgive me for killing a man to save my own life."

"Gia!" Darling said. "That's not how it is."

"Sure seems that way to me."

"I'm sorry," Darling said in a quiet voice.

"And why didn't you defend me?"

"Oh, honey, I did. You know I did."

And I knew she was right. Why had I ever doubted her?

"When you coming home?"

I looked around. I was done here. "Tonight," I said.

"Let's do lunch tomorrow. I'll come over and we'll figure out where to go from there."

"I'm looking forward to it," I said and meant it.

I hung up the phone. How come it felt so devastating to have Mrs. Parks and her god-fearing church family angry at me?

It truly felt awful. But I wasn't going to cry about it this time. I hadn't lost a daughter. Mrs. Parks was allowed to feel whatever she felt.

I was able to get on the next flight back to the city and woke the next day excited to see Darling.

I'd told the staff downstairs to let Darling up via my private elevator.

I opened the door with a smile that immediately disappeared and was replaced by shock.

Mrs. Parks stood outside my door.

"May I come in?" she asked.

I nodded. Seeing her standing there with a sweet smile on her face was a lot.

I found myself unable to speak and biting back tears.

She followed me in, and I invited her to sit at the table. "I just made some coffee. Would you like some?"

"I'd love some."

She sat at the table primly and put her handbag on the chair next to her.

It all felt so formal.

"I came today to see if you would consider being on the board of a foundation I've started in Clara's memory."

"Of course," I said immediately.

"Wonderful," she said and smiled.

We both sat there in silence for a few seconds. Then I had to say something.

"Does that mean you forgive me?"

"Oh, Gia," she said, reaching for my hand and squeezing it tightly. "I forgave you the instant it happened. I was just angry at the circumstances. Not you. The small hope I'd been holding onto since Clara's death was that somehow, some way her death would be for good. And in my mind, I kept envisioning that somehow her death would stop others from dying."

I nodded.

"So when Phillips was killed, it seemed that there was just another death resulting from Clara's passing instead of her death saving lives. It got all confused in my mind, and I lashed out. I never meant for you to think I didn't forgive you or understand. When Darling told me it took me a day or two to unravel all those emotions and realize what I really was upset about.

The second I did, I called Darling and said that I needed to speak to you immediately. I've been calling Darling every day, asking when you would be back in town."

I blinked back tears.

"Well, I'd be happy to serve on your board in any capacity you'd like," I said.

"Oh good!" she said and clapped her hands before standing up. "I have to run, but I would be honored if you would come to Sunday dinner at my house this week. We would love to have you. Darling will be there, of course. It's just a small gathering for family only."

I hesitated.

"Are you sure, you just said 'family only'..." I trailed off.

She smiled. "Oh honey, you're family now. You risked your life to help us. If that's not family then I don't know what is. We'll see you Sunday then, okay?"

I nodded, afraid that if I spoke I'd start to cry.

But as soon as the door closed behind her, the tears came.

The End

Stay up to date with Kristi Belcamino's new releases by scanning the QR code below!

(You'll receive a **free** copy of *First Vengeance: A Gia Santella Prequel!*)

Did you enjoy *Deadly Lies?* Scan the QR code below to let us know your thoughts!

ALSO BY KRISTI BELCAMINO

Enjoying Kristi Belcamino? Scan the code below to see her Amazon Author page!

Gia Santella Crime Thriller Series

Vendetta

Vigilante

Vengeance

Black Widow

Day of the Dead

Border Line

Night Fall

Stone Cold

Cold as Death

Cold Blooded

Dark Shadows

Dark Vengeance

Dark Justice

Deadly Justice

Deadly Lies

Additional books in series:

Taste of Vengeance

Lone Raven

Vigilante Crime Series

Blood & Roses

Blood & Fire

Blood & Bone

Blood & Tears

Queen of Spades Thrillers

Queen of Spades

The One-Eyed Jack

The Suicide King

The Ace of Clubs

The Joker

The Wild Card

High Stakes

Poker Face

Standalone Novels

Coming For You

Sanctuary City

The Girl in the River

Buried Secrets

Dead Wrong (Young Adult Mystery)

Gabriella Giovanni Mystery Series

Blessed are the Dead

Blessed are the Meek

Blessed are Those Who Weep

Blessed are Those Who Mourn

Blessed are the Peacemakers

Blessed are the Merciful

Nonfiction

Letters from a Serial Killer

ALSO BY WITHOUT WARRANT

More Thriller Series from Without Warrant Authors

Dana Gray Mysteries by C.J. Cross

Girl Left Behind

Girl on the Hill

Girl in the Grave

The Kenzie Gilmore Series by Biba Pearce

Afterburn

Dead Heat

Heatwave

Burnout

Deep Heat

Fever Pitch

Storm Surge (Coming Soon)

Willow Grace FBI Thrillers by Anya Mora

Shadow of Grace

Condition of Grace (Coming Soon)

Gia Santella Crime Thriller Series

by Kristi Belcamino

Vendetta

Vigilante

Vengeance

Black Widow

Day of the Dead

Border Line

Night Fall

Stone Cold

Cold as Death

Cold Blooded

Dark Shadows

Dark Vengeance

Dark Justice

Deadly Justice

Deadly Lies

Vigilante Crime Series by Kristi Belcamino

Blood & Roses

Blood & Fire

Blood & Bone

Blood & Tears

Queen of Spades Thrillers by Kristi Belcamino

Queen of Spades

The One-Eyed Jack

The Suicide King

The Ace of Clubs

The Joker

The Wild Card

High Stakes

Poker Face

AUTHOR'S NOTE

When I was 16, I read Jackie Collins' book, *Lucky*, and it rocked my world. For the first time in my prolific reading life (yes, I was the kid holed up in my room reading as many books as I could as often as I could), I met a character who was not only Italian-American like me, but a strong, powerful, and successful badass woman who didn't take crap from anybody and loved to have sex!

Although I had dreamed of being a writer, it never seemed like a realistic dream and my attempts at writing seemed pitiful. So I studied journalism and became a reporter—it was a way to be a writer and have a steady paycheck.

It was only when I was in my forties that I got the guts to write a book. And it was a few years after that I was brave enough to write the character I really wanted to write—Gia Santella.

She's not Lucky Santangelo, of course. I mean, nobody could be as cool as Lucky is, but I like to think that maybe Gia and Lucky would have been friends.

Gia is my alter ego. The woman who does and says things I never could or would, but whom I admire and would love to be friends with.

If you like her, I'm pretty sure we'd be the best of friends in real life!

x Kristi

ABOUT THE AUTHOR

Kristi Belcamino is a USA Today bestseller, an Agatha, Anthony, Barry & Macavity finalist, and an Italian Mama who bakes a tasty biscotti.

Her books feature strong, kickass, independent women facing unspeakable evil in order to seek justice for those unable to do so themselves.

In her former life, as an award-winning crime reporter at newspapers in California, she flew over Big Sur in an FA-18 jet with the Blue Angels, raced a Dodge Viper at Laguna Seca, attended barbecues at the morgue, and conversed with serial killers.

During her decade covering crime, Belcamino wrote and reported about many high-profile cases including the Laci Peterson murder and Chandra Levy disappearance. She has appeared on *Inside Edition* and local television shows. She now writes fiction and works part-time as a reporter covering the police beat for the St. Paul *Pioneer Press*.

Her work has appeared in such prominent publications as *Salon*, the *Miami Herald*, *San Jose Mercury News,* and *Chicago Tribune*.

facebook.com/kristibelcaminowriter
instagram.com/kristibelcaminobooks
tiktok.com/@kristibelcaminobooks

Printed in the USA
CPSIA information can be obtained
at www.ICGtesting.com
LVHW020841051124
795747LV00015B/717